"Don't touch me! I'm not one of your possessions, Zeke."

Marianne continued. "I'm your wife."

"Dead right you're my wife," Zeke grated slowly. "So why don't you start acting like it?"

"You arrogant—"

"You're my wife, I'm your husband, so what's got into you all of a sudden?"

Before she could answer, he had taken her mouth in a kiss that immediately ignited a response deep in the core of her. He only had to touch her and she melted for him. But she *had* to resist him, she had to make him understand....

HELEN BROOKS lives in Northamptonshire, England, and is married with three children. As she is a committed Christian, busy housewife and mother, her spare time is at a premium, but her hobbies include reading, swimming, gardening and walking her two energetic, inquisitive and very endearing young dogs. Her long-cherished aspiration to write became a reality when she put pen to paper on reaching the age of forty, and sent the result off to Harlequin Mills & Boon.

Look out for *The Irresistible Tycoon*
by Helen Brooks
on-sale June 2002 (#2256)

Books by Helen Brooks

Helen Brooks

A WHIRLWIND MARRIAGE

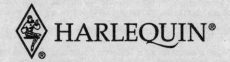

HARLEQUIN®

TORONTO • NEW YORK • LONDON
AMSTERDAM • PARIS • SYDNEY • HAMBURG
STOCKHOLM • ATHENS • TOKYO • MILAN • MADRID
PRAGUE • WARSAW • BUDAPEST • AUCKLAND

ISBN 0-373-12237-3

A WHIRLWIND MARRIAGE

First North American Publication 2002.

CHAPTER ONE

ZEKE BUCHANAN glanced at his wife as he rose from the breakfast table, but although Marianne was aware of his gaze she didn't raise her head from her contemplation of the contents of her coffee cup, not even when he stopped just behind her and rested his hands on her slender shoulders as he said, 'You haven't forgotten the Mortons are coming at seven?'

No, she hadn't forgotten the Mortons. She steeled herself to show no reaction, either in her body or her voice, when she replied coolly, 'No, of course not. Everything's in order.'

'Good.' There was a moment's hesitation, and then he bent and placed a swift kiss on the top of her blond head. 'I probably won't be home much before seven myself. I'm flying up to Stoke this morning to look at an old factory site I'm interested in, but I should be back by mid-afternoon if you need me.'

If I need you? Of course I need you, but that's a concept that's alien to you, isn't it? She didn't trust the bitterness not to show if she spoke, so she merely nodded without turning her head to look at him.

'Goodbye, Marianne.'

His voice was cold now, and she replied in like vein when she said, 'Goodbye, Zeke.'

And then the breakfast room door had shut behind him and she was alone. She sat absolutely still for a full minute, willing herself not to give way to the tears that were always threatening these days, and then she rose very slowly and walked across to the huge, south-facing window which took up most of one wall.

The vista beyond the glass was a breathtaking aerial view of half of London, or so it seemed. The penthouse, at the top of a high-rise block of luxury flats, had been tailormade for Zeke long before he had met her, more than two years ago. It was the last word in opulent living, from the massive drawing room regally decorated in blue and gold to the sumptuous master bedroom and its decadent *en suite* bathroom, which was black and silver and mirrored from floor to ceiling. And Marianne hated it. She loathed it.

She knew one of Zeke's old girlfriends—a very successful and glamorous redhead by the exotic name of Liliana de Giraud, who was *the* interior designer to the rich and famous—had designed the penthouse, and once she had discovered that some twelve months ago her dislike of the brazen bachelor pad had turned to revulsion.

She had lost count of how many times she had asked Zeke to come with her to look at different properties—some apartments, some houses—but always he had fobbed her off with 'tomorrow'. But tomorrow had never come.

She relaxed against the window for a moment, her forehead pressed against the cold glass, and then she straightened abruptly, drawing her shoulders back military-style and lifting her small chin determinedly.

None of that! she told herself silently. You're not going to give in to the urge to run and hide. They were going through a bad patch, but that didn't mean she had to fold under the pressure. She would come through this; she would. She had coped with the shock of her mother's sudden death four years ago—she would cope with this. But, oh... She bit her lip hard. What she would give to talk to her mother now, just to be able to tell someone all of it.

She felt she would go mad sometimes, cut off from the world in this ivory tower Zeke had created.

And then, as though in answer to the silent desperate plea, the telephone rang. Marianne let it ring until the answer-machine cut in. The only people who rang these days were Zeke, one or other of their social circle, or business acquaintances, and she didn't feel like talking to any of those.

'Hi, Marianne. Long time no talkie! This is Pat—Patricia—in case you haven't guessed, and as I'm up in town for a day or two I thought I'd—'

Pat's voice was cut off as Marianne lifted the receiver and said breathlessly, 'Pat? Oh, Pat. It's so lovely to hear your voice.'

'Is it? You only had to pick up the phone any day to hear it, Annie,' Pat said with a chuckle to soften the admonishment.

Marianne blinked and then found herself smiling. The same old straightforward Pat. It was her friend's habit of plain speaking that had got under Zeke's skin even before he had met Pat, and the two had never hit it off. Pat was right, though; she should have contacted her before this, Marianne told herself silently. But with all that was happening between Zeke and herself she had felt—ridiculously, perhaps—that it would be a betrayal of her husband. She didn't feel like that any more. Not since last night.

'You're in town?' Marianne said now. 'Can we meet up for lunch or something?'

'Great. Do you want me to come round to the apartment?' Pat asked briskly.

Marianne glanced round the suffocatingly exquisite interior and shut her eyes tightly for a second before she said, 'No, we'll eat out. My treat. There's a great little

French place a few blocks away: Rochelle's, in St Martin's Street. I'll meet you there at twelve if that's okay?'

'Terrific. See you then. And, Annie—?'

'Yes?' she asked carefully.

'Are you all right?'

Marianne took a deep breath and said quietly, 'No, no I'm not all right, Pat.'

'Didn't think you were. Twelve, then.' And in characteristic fashion the phone went dead.

Oh, Pat. Marianne replaced the receiver and stood staring at the telephone for some moments as a great flood of relief and expectation swept through her. She hadn't realised just how much she needed Pat's down-to-earth common sense and no-frills approach to life until this very second, but now she couldn't wait to see her.

She glanced at the small gold wristwatch Zeke had given her for her twenty-first birthday, a few months after she had married him. Eight o'clock. Four hours to go. But suddenly the day which had stretched endlessly in front of her just minutes before had been transformed.

A long, hot soak in the bath. Marianne nodded to the thought, and, leaving the breakfast table just as it was, walked through to one of the two guest bedrooms which both had their own *en suites*.

She rarely used the master bedroom's *en suite*—even though it boasted an Olympian Jacuzzi bath—unless Zeke was around, and then she only did it to avoid yet another row. She couldn't quite explain it, but the flamboyant, lavish black-and-silver bathroom always seemed to emphasise everything that was wrong in their marriage and just how far they had grown apart in two years.

She was still in her silk nightie and négligé, and now she discarded the flimsy wisps of material on the floor as she ran herself a bath liberally doused with expensive oils.

Once in the warm, silky water she lay back with a soft sigh, and for the first time in months allowed her mind to drift back to how it had been when she had first told Pat about Zeke. In spite of the direness of her present situation a small smile played round her mouth as she recalled Pat's words.

'And all this has happened in the eight weeks I've been in Canada?' Pat's voice had been distinctly miffed. 'But nothing *ever* happens in Bridgeton, Annie.'

'What can I say?' She'd been smiling as she'd taken in her friend's woebegone face. 'He came, he saw, he conquered. Zeke's like that.'

'And he's rich *and* good-looking?' It had been almost a wail. 'Tell me he's got a brother, *please*.'

'Oh, Pat.' She had been openly laughing, but as she'd stared into the pretty face of her best friend—the girl she'd grown up with and who lived just a few hundred yards away—she'd admitted to a secret feeling of amazement herself.

That Zeke Buchanan, millionaire property developer and entrepreneur extraordinaire, should have fallen in love with her *was* something fairy tales were made of. And it had all happened so quickly.

She'd glanced down at the enormous cluster of diamonds on the third finger of her left hand and felt the same giddy rush of excitement as when Zeke had placed it there seven days before.

A whirlwind romance. Everyone, *everyone* was talking about it—the whole village had been agog that a girl from their little backwater should have caught a big fish from the capital. But she had. He loved her and she loved him, more than life itself.

She'd raised misty eyes to Pat's fascinated face as her friend had said, 'I want to hear every little morsel, all right? From the first time you laid eyes on him until he put that great whopper of a ring on your finger. *Everything*, mind! There was little old me thinking *I* was having a good time in Canada when instead it was all happening at home! I can't believe it. I really can't believe it. That'll teach me to go camping in the mountains for weeks on end—the most I saw was a moose and the rear end of a bear.'

'But you did have a good time?'

'I thought I had.' Pat's face had been comical. 'But compared to you... So, come on, spill the beans.'

'There isn't really much to tell.' They had been standing on the doorstep of her father's rambling old house, and she had drawn Pat into the hall before leading the way through to the large country kitchen at the back of the aged property. There she had said, 'Zeke came to have a look at that land on the outskirts of the village, Farnon's Farm, that's been designated for housing and a new school and so on. He was driving through the main street—in his Ferrari,' she'd added as she turned round from putting the kettle on and dimpled at Pat, who'd given an envious groan, 'when he saw me leaving the village shop.'

'And?'

Marianne had turned back to fix the coffee tray and Pat had grabbed hold of her arms as she'd said, 'Leave the flipping coffee, for goodness' sake, Annie, and *tell* me!' determinedly pushing her down in one of the straight-backed chairs placed neatly round the huge old kitchen table.

'And he stopped and introduced himself and we chatted for a while, and then he asked me out to dinner that night,' Marianne had said matter-of-factly, clasping her hands together in her lap. 'And then we just started seeing each other.'

And she had been transported into another realm, another dimension, a place where even the most ordinary, mundane aspects of living took on a thrilling quality because Zeke loved her.

'You jammy, jammy thing.' Pat had exhaled very slowly. 'But I have to say if anyone deserves a decent break it's you, Annie. There's not many girls with your intelligence and looks that would have given up the chance of university and spreading their wings to keep house for their father, not to mention taking on the job as general dogsbody at the surgery.'

'It's not like that. I enjoy what I do,' Marianne had responded quickly as she'd stood up to make the coffee.

'Hmph!' The exclamation had said it all.

The two girls had been bosom friends from when they could toddle, and the fact that they were both only children and their birthdays were just days apart had meant they had tackled all the important childhood milestones together.

Nursery school, big school, youth club—the two of them had braved each one hand in hand, and Pat, more than anyone else in the world, knew how hard it had been when Marianne's beloved mother had died horribly suddenly of a brain haemorrhage just as Marianne had been set to leave for university two years before.

Josh Kirby, Marianne's father, had been devastated, and she had had to bear the added weight of seeing her normally cool and composed doctor father go to pieces on top of her own consuming grief.

Marianne's mother had been receptionist, secretary and—as Pat had pointed out—general dogsbody in Josh's small but busy surgery, which was situated in the front of their house, and Marianne had known what she had to do within days of her mother's passing.

She had put all thoughts of university on hold and made

things as normal and easy as she could for her grief-
stricken father, stepping quietly and efficiently into her
mother's shoes both domestically and in the surgery. And
she had had her reward over the next twenty-four months
as she'd watched her father's pain and anguish diminish
and he'd slowly come to terms with his loss.

Marianne hadn't regretted her decision to stay, not for
a minute—a second—but it had been hard sometimes
when she'd heard Pat and other members of their set talking about all they'd done and seen when they came home
for the holidays, whilst she'd been stuck in Bridgeton
where the most exciting thing that happened was Ned
Riley getting drunk on a Friday night and dancing his way
home.

But then Zeke had happened. Zeke Buchanan, with his
jet-black hair and smoky grey eyes that had had the power
to melt her with just one glance.

Marianne shivered suddenly, reaching forward and turning on the hot tap although the water wasn't really cool—
the chill came from within rather than from without. Once
the water was steaming, and as hot as she could stand it,
she relaxed again, and almost immediately she was back
in Bridgeton in that long hot summer of two years before.

'I hope he knows how lucky he is, your Zeke.' Pat had
smiled at her and she'd smiled back. 'You're one in a
million, and I don't just mean your looks either. You're
nice inside, Annie, where it really counts.'

'You couldn't be just a tiny bit prejudiced, could you?'

She remembered she'd laughed softly before she'd said,
passing Pat a mug of steaming coffee, 'And you will be
my bridesmaid?'

'Just try and stop me.' Pat had wrinkled her small snub
nose appreciatively as she'd drawn in the heady aroma of
rich coffee beans. 'Have you set a date yet?'

She'd taken a deep breath. She hadn't been sure of how Pat would react to the news. 'The second Saturday in October.'

'Next year, you mean.'

'This year.'

'This year?' Pat had jerked up straighter, shooting coffee all over her white top, chosen specifically to show off her deep Canadian tan. 'But that's only—'

'Six weeks away. Yes, I know.' She had forced a smile. Everyone, *everyone* had behaved as though she was planning to do something immoral rather than marry the man she loved. 'Zeke doesn't want to wait and neither do I. He can afford to pay to have everything brought swiftly together. He's booked the reception at this wonderful London hotel, and the cars and the flowers and everything. And the church in the village is free, so...'

'But your dress. *My* dress?'

'That's no problem. Zeke's on first-name terms with several designers, and one of them—' she'd mentioned a name that had brought Pat's green eyes opening wider '—has just finished a special collection for a show in Paris all to do with weddings. One of the dresses—oh, Pat, you ought to see it—is just *gorgeous*, and he's agreed to do your dress, too. So you see, everything is sorted.'

Pat's lips had still been agape and she'd suddenly become aware of it, shutting her mouth with a little snap as she'd leant back in her seat with her eyes glued on Marianne's face. 'And you are sure, you're absolutely sure this is what you want?' she'd asked slowly.

'Absolutely.'

'I hate to be the original wet blanket, but have you considered that little phrase, "Marry in haste, repent at leisure"?' Pat had asked almost apologetically.

'No need.' Her voice had been firm. 'I've never been

more sure about anything in my life than I am about marrying Zeke.'

Marianne sat up straight suddenly, swishing the water into a foamy wave that sloshed over the side of the bath onto the ankle-deep carpeting below. And she *had* been sure, one hundred per cent sure, that she and Zeke were going to be blissfully content and happy ever after, she told herself, wrapping a massive fluffy bath sheet round her sarong-style and padding through to the master bedroom.

Once seated at her dressing table, she glanced at the row of costly perfume bottles and the set of mother-of-pearl jewellery boxes dripping with expensive items of jewellery without really seeing them, her mind winging back in time again.

She had repeated that conversation with Pat to Zeke word for word when he'd arrived to take her out to dinner later the same day.

Since the first afternoon they had met Zeke had insisted on driving down from London to her home village on the outskirts of Tunbridge Wells every evening, claiming that the thirty-plus miles from his offices in Lewisham barely gave the Ferrari time for a workout.

And she hadn't tried to dissuade him *too* hard, she admitted to herself now, in spite of worrying about him dashing backwards and forwards each day. She had needed to see him every evening, to feel his strong arms about her, his lips on hers. He had been like a drug, a sensual, handsome, powerful and wildly intoxicating drug. He still was. Although now she understood that the very thing you craved above all else could carry a crushing price with it.

She should have known, from his reaction when she had innocently prattled on about Pat, that a serpent was rearing its head in her Garden of Eden.

'So, our bridesmaid tried to warn you off me?' Zeke had asked with dry amusement, his smoky grey eyes creasing at the edges as he'd smiled at her briefly before concentrating on the country road along which they'd been travelling. 'I'll have to have a word with her some time.'

There had been something, the slightest inflexion in his deep voice, that had suggested he wasn't quite so amused by Pat's cautionary advice as he'd seemed to be, and Marianne had glanced at the hard, handsome profile for a moment before she'd said, 'She didn't mean anything by it, Zeke. Pat's just a little protective of me, I guess, since Mum died.'

'She doesn't need to be,' he had answered lightly, but still with the slight edge to his voice. 'I'm all the protection you need.'

She didn't need any protection—she was more than capable of taking care of herself!

The words had hovered on her lips but she'd bitten them back—probably a grave mistake in hindsight, she thought now—but she'd been unwilling to spoil the lovely summer evening by prolonging what had suddenly become an awkward conversation. Their first awkward conversation.

'Pat will see how it is the moment she meets you,' she had said instead, as she listened to the voice of love telling her he had raced down from London after a hectic, long day—he was always at his office by seven in the morning—and she couldn't expect him not to be a little tetchy now and again. And perhaps she'd been unwise to repeat the conversation with Pat. But she'd thought he'd laugh at the ridiculous notion that their love could waver, like she had. Still, men viewed these things differently, especially strong, decisive, capable men like Zeke.

She'd known he was as resilient and tough as they came; he'd had to be with the background he had come from.

Abandoned by his single parent mother when he was just a few months old, he had spent most of his childhood in and out of foster homes, with two attempts at adoption failing. But he'd had a brilliant mind and an even more formidable will, and at the age of eighteen—armed with four grade A A-levels—he had decided to put himself through university, studying every day and working every night and weekend to pay his way.

Three years later he had emerged into the world again with a first-class degree, and after two years of working all hours of the day and night he had earnt himself enough capital to start his own business.

That had been the start of a spectacularly swift climb to wealth and power which had made him—at the age of thirty-five—one of the richest men in his field.

Wise investments, shrewd business deals, ruthless take-overs and a reputation that he wasn't someone to mess with had assured him of a place at the very top of the tree, and if she hadn't seen the real Zeke—the tender, ardent lover and fascinating intellectual—he would have scared her to death.

But all she'd known at their first meeting, in the village street on a sunny July afternoon full of the scents of summer, was that the most amazing, magnetic man she had ever met wanted to take her out to dinner. And, at direct variance with her shy, reserved, gentle nature, she had answered eagerly in the affirmative. And so it had begun.

The sudden jarring call of the telephone cut in on her thoughts, and more out of habit than anything she rose and padded through to the breakfast room, where the answer-machine was situated.

'Marianne?' It was Zeke's voice, impatient and slightly irritated. 'Pick up the phone.'

Her hand was actually halfway to the receiver when she

stopped herself. Why did she always do what he said? she asked herself as her stomach lurched and trembled. She was a full-grown woman with a mind of her own. She didn't *have* to pick up the phone if she didn't want to.

'Marianne?' The deep dark voice was definitely terse now, and she pictured him in her mind's eye, frowning at the inoffensive plastic that had dared to thwart him. 'Hell, I haven't got time for this. Are you in the bath or something? Look, I just wanted to check you've remembered to order that pâté Gerald Morton likes so much, the one from Harrods. I was going to remind you last night, but with all that happened—' He stopped abruptly. 'Anyway, get them to send some round if you haven't done so already.'

She waited for a word of goodbye, something, *anything*, but there was just the sound of the receiver being replaced.

'Damn Gerald Morton's pâté.' It was soft at first, and then she said it louder, her voice shaking, *'Damn the rotten pâté!'* Their marriage was falling apart and he was worrying about a dinner party!

Purposefully now, she walked through to the beautiful drawing room to stand in front of the ornate fireplace above which hung their huge wedding portrait.

She ignored the young, glowing-faced girl on Zeke's arm and stared instead at the tall dark figure of her husband, at the midnight-black hair cut severely short, which just emphasised his rugged appeal tenfold when added to the harsh, handsome face, the jawline square and uncompromising.

But it was his eyes that had first enchanted her that day two years ago. Grey, and of a warm smoky quality, they had floored her. Absolutely floored her. They still did.

When she had looked into his eyes during the early days of their relationship it hadn't mattered that they came from vastly different worlds. Zeke from a rags-to-riches background and a childhood devoid of love and stability, and she from a steady, non-eventful middle-class upbringing full of love and family values.

She had been only twenty when she'd met Zeke and had been sexually unawakened; he had had relationships with women from the age of sixteen and had been a cynical and worldly-wise thirty-five.

He hadn't kissed her until their second date, however, the evening after the first day they'd met. But when he had drawn her into his arms in the intimate shadows inside her garden gate she had known why the fumbling attentions of her previous boyfriends had merely irritated and slightly disgusted her.

The subtle, spicy flavour of his aftershave, the hard lean body and devastating male sensuality had shaken her to her roots. By the time the kiss had finished she'd been trembling with passion and excitement, her heartbeat thudding in her ears and the blood rushing through her veins like hot mulled wine.

'You're special, Marianne.' Zeke had pulled her closer into him as he had spoken, wrapping his arms around her as if to bind her to him. 'Very, very special.'

She hadn't been able to speak, she'd barely been able to stand, and when his mouth had taken hers again in a kiss that was powerful and hungry she'd responded wildly, knowing she hadn't really been alive until that moment.

She had known by the end of that first week that she loved him and that she couldn't live without him, the intensity of her love as frightening as it was thrilling.

The bath sheet slipped a little and she caught it to her, her eyes never leaving the cool, handsome face of her husband.

And when she had married him she had given him all

of herself—body, soul and spirit—withholding nothing. *Fool, fool, fool.*

Pat was waiting for her when Marianne walked into the elegant and tranquil confines of Rochelle's, and she was glad she had thought to ring in advance and reserve a table for two in her name. Or rather Zeke's name, she thought a trifle bitterly. The magic name that opened myriad doors.

'Annie!' Pat bounced to her feet, her thick brown curls bobbing as she waved enthusiastically, as though the restaurant was crowded and busy instead of being virtually empty. In another half an hour, though, that would all change, and by one o'clock every table would be occupied. But for now it was blessedly quiet and private.

'Oh, Pat, it's so *good* to see you,' Marianne breathed as the two exchanged a bear hug.

'And you.' Pat grinned at her as they sat down, and then, as the waiter appeared at their side like a rabbit out of a hat, she said, 'You still drinking the same? Dry martini, wasn't it?'

'I prefer a glass of wine these days.' She didn't add that Zeke had educated her on good wines until now she could hold her own with the best wine waiter. 'Red is your preference, isn't it?'

Pat nodded. 'Not much changes,' she said with a wry grimace.

Oh, if only that were true. Marianne selected a superior bottle of wine that she knew from experience was soft and mellow with a warm oak flavour, and then, once the two girls were alone again, she said softly, 'You look terrific, Pat.'

'So do you.' Pat's pretty, pert face was unusually soft as she surveyed Marianne's slender, finely boned figure and beautiful heart-shaped face, the huge cornflower-blue eyes, small straight nose and full mouth framed by a mass of luxuriant silver-blonde hair that hung in silky waves to below Marianne's shoulderblades. 'But you're too thin, if you don't mind me saying so, and with you that means you're worrying or unhappy about something. You've never eaten for comfort like me, have you?'

Marianne shook her head slowly. You never got any pussy-footing around with Pat, and after all the sycophantic boot-lickers that tried to attach themselves to Zeke's brilliant black star, her friend's frankness was refreshing to say the least.

'So, what gives?' Pat asked gently.

The return of the wine waiter delayed Marianne's answer somewhat, but once they were sitting with an enormous glass of red wine and an embossed menu in front of each of them, Marianne said without any preamble, 'It's all such a mess, Pat—me, Zeke, everything. I thought…I thought it was going to be so different. I knew his work was a big part of his life, and that's all right, it is really, but he doesn't seem to understand that I need something to do. I can't just be content with keeping house and lunches with the wives of his friends and shopping afternoons and organising dinner parties and so on. I'm not made like that.'

'Nor me,' Pat said with a shudder.

'He's expected all the compromise to be on my side. I've had to fit completely into his world, and he hasn't made the slightest attempt to fit into mine. He doesn't want me to work, says I don't need to, and even when I tried to set up some voluntary work at the local hospital he made it so difficult I finished up letting it go. The apartment…I feel it's a prison, I hate it, and he promised before we got married that we'd leave there as soon as we found somewhere more suitable for bringing up a family.'

'A family?' Pat queried carefully.

Marianne stared at her miserably. 'It just hasn't happened,' she said quietly. 'The first twelve months it didn't matter, but then I started to worry, so we went for tests and everything's fine, apparently, but still no baby. And this constant city life, it's stifling me, Pat. Choking me.'

'Have you told him all this?' said Pat, watching her closely.

Marianne nodded. 'But he has an answer for everything, he's that sort of man, and I always end up feeling in the wrong. The doctor at the hospital…he thought I wasn't getting pregnant because I was stressed, and when he said that it was more reason for Zeke to say he doesn't want me to do anything outside the home. I tried to tell him it was *because* I was being locked away from the outside I was stressed, but he wouldn't accept it.'

'Because he didn't want to,' Pat said astutely. She'd had a taste of Zeke Buchanan's single-mindedness when he had all but shut her out of Marianne's life once they were married.

'I still love him, Pat.' Marianne was staring down into her glass as she spoke and missed Pat's green eyes narrowing shrewdly on her unhappy face. 'But then last night we had a terrible row.'

She raised her head then, and the stark misery in the azure blue eyes took Pat's breath away. But before she could say anything the waiter was at their side for their lunch order, and once he had gone Marianne changed the subject, insisting on hearing all Pat's news, and how she was progressing in her job as surgery nurse at the local veterinary practice in Bridgeton.

It was as they finished their first course it happened. Pat had just eaten the last mouthful of her avocado and prawn cocktail—one of Rochelle's specialities—and had leant forward across the table, saying quietly, 'Annie, have you told your father how things are?' when she became aware her friend's eyes were transfixed at a point over her shoulder.

'Oh, Pat.' It was the merest thread of a whisper, but as Pat made to turn in her chair Marianne said urgently, 'No, don't turn round, whatever you do, and talk—talk about anything, quickly.'

Pat had always been the person you could most depend on to rise to any emergency, and as she obediently began to prattle about one of the veterinary surgery's most amusing patients, Marianne forced her eyes away from the little party who had just come into the restaurant and on to the perplexed face of her friend. But on the perimeter of her vision she saw a tall, dark figure stop abruptly and then, as an obliging waiter showed the party to their seats, leave the others and start to make his way across towards them. He had seen her.

'Marianne?' Pat's voice was cut off as though by a knife as Zeke's deep drawl sounded just behind her. 'You didn't tell me you had a luncheon date.'

'Hallo, Zeke.' Marianne was amazed to find her voice was perfectly calm and composed. 'Pat only phoned me this morning to tell me she was in town so I didn't know.'

Pat had turned in her seat by this time, and as cool grey eyes met bright green Zeke smiled coldly, before he said, 'Pat, I didn't know it was you. How are you?'

'I'm fine, Zeke.' Pat had never been one for flowery effusion, but even so it was succinct in the extreme.

'I'm sure you are.' It was neither condemnatory or approving, and Zeke's grey eyes took on all the warmth of cold granite as he nodded in abrupt dismissal of the other woman before turning to Marianne again. 'I'll see you later,' he said smoothly. 'Did you get my message before you left?'

'Your...?' And then she remembered. Gerald Morton's pâté! 'Yes, Zeke,' she said steadily. 'I got your message.'

He looked impossibly handsome as he stood there, his ebony hair sleek and shining and immaculate and the big, lean body clothed in a beautifully cut suit that couldn't disguise the leashed strength of the hard, masculine frame. Deep grooves splayed out from either side of his straight nose to his mouth, a mouth which very rarely smiled except with mocking amusement, and the uncompromisingly severe quality of his dark good looks was tantalisingly at odds with the sensual knowledge in the darkly lashed grey eyes.

And he was a sensuous lover, lustful and imaginative, but with a sensitivity and tenderness to his lovemaking that made her—even with all that was wrong between them—*ache* to be in his arms whenever they were alone.

'Excuse me. This is a business lunch and there's plenty to get through.' There was a message in the cool, even tone that was for Marianne alone, but she merely stared back at him, her eyes steady and her small chin uplifted.

And then he turned, walking back to his table without another word and without glancing their way again.

This time Marianne didn't stop Pat when her friend turned round and made a swift, but thorough assessment of Zeke's companions. The two men Pat glanced over, but the green eyes stopped on the fourth figure at the table, who was engaging Zeke in animated conversation and totally ignoring their colleagues, and remained there for a full thirty seconds before Pat settled herself back in her seat.

Marianne answered the question Pat was too tactful to ask. 'She's Liliana de Giraud,' she said flatly. 'You might have heard of her? She's the hottest interior designer around.'

Why, oh, why hadn't she considered the possibility that Zeke might come here for lunch? She knew it was his favourite eating place in the lunch hour when he was entertaining clients and such, but he had said he was going to fly to Stoke and wouldn't be back until mid-afternoon. Had that been a lie? Had he been intending to take Liliana out for lunch all along?

'She's full of herself.' Pat's down-to-earth evaluation was spoken scathingly.

'That's because she's very pleased with life at the moment,' Marianne said painfully. 'Zeke has just acquired her services for a massive development deal that will provide luxury homes for the élite in one of the best parts of London. Apparently he was very fortunate to get her.'

'Oh, yes?'

'Of course the fact that they were lovers for a while five years ago might have swayed her agreement, added to which she still wants him…badly.' Marianne's voice was expressionless, with a flatness that spoke of deep hurt. 'She had made that very clear to me several times when we've met socially.'

'This was the cause of that row last night?' Pat asked in sudden understanding.

Marianne nodded with a brittle smile. 'Zeke thinks I'm being over-emotional,' she said evenly. And this from the man who didn't like her dancing with another male—even one of his friends—and who objected if he thought she was spending too long in conversation with any one man at the various social functions they attended.

'And you're sure you're not?' Pat probed gently.

Marianne's lovely deep blue eyes took on a bleakness that was an answer in itself. 'Oh, I'm sure, Pat,' she said quietly. 'I'm not the jealous type—' unlike Zeke '—but Liliana has gone to great pains to let me know how much she hates me. Never in front of Zeke, of course, she's all sweetness and light when he's around, but she wants him back and she doesn't care what she does to get him. She's the master of innuendo and acid jibes coated in sugar towards her own sex, but the men just can't see it. I don't know one woman who is comfortable with her.'

'I'm not surprised,' Pat said drily.

In the first heady days of her marriage she hadn't been threatened by Liliana de Giraud's manoeuvrings, in fact she had even felt sorry for the other woman and had tentatively offered her the hand of friendship before Liliana's covert hostility had made her aware she was likely to get it bitten off. So much for magnanimity, Marianne thought wretchedly, allowing herself one glance across the room and then wishing she hadn't as she saw Zeke and Liliana's heads close together. She had been innocent, far, far too innocent, when she had married Zeke.

She forced herself to eat all of her lunch with every appearance of enjoyment, and although she didn't glance over at the other table again her heightened senses made her aware of each time Liliana looked their way.

By unspoken mutual consent she and Pat lingered over their liqueur coffees—Marianne hadn't relished the thought of passing Zeke's table on their way out—and so it was that Zeke left first. She acknowledged his raised hand of farewell with a nod and a cool smile, and then tensed as she saw Liliana reach up and speak in Zeke's ear before beginning to make her way over.

'Liliana's coming.'

It was all she managed to say to Pat before the redhead came within earshot, and then in the next moment she was engulfed in a cloud of expensive, sultry perfume as Liliana bent to brush her cheek with cool lips, gushing, 'Sweetie, how lovely to see you. We didn't know you'd be lunching with your little friend today.'

'Hallo, Liliana.' Marianne was eternally grateful for the fortifying effects of the excellent meal—not to mention the wine and liqueur coffee—as she looked up into the redhead's ice-blue eyes. 'This is Pat, by the way. Pat, Liliana.'

The 'little friend' didn't smile, neither did she bother to speak as she inclined her head, but the green eyes narrowed with such naked feline coldness that it actually seemed to take Liliana aback a little. She wasn't used to such overt honesty.

'I must dash.' Liliana turned back to Marianne, her exquisitely creamy skin—which went with her vibrant hair—flushed from the effect of Pat's scrutiny. 'Zeke and I have *heaps* to discuss. We're going to be tied up for days on this project, so you'll have to be brave in doing without him, sweetie.'

'Will I?' Marianne called on all her father's stoical, imperturbable genes and her mother's poised, self-possessed ones as she smiled with a serenity she was far from feeling and said, 'I'll have to make sure we spoil each other when we're together, then, won't I, Liliana?'

The cruel, self-assured smile that had been hovering on the red-painted lips vanished for a second before it was immediately brought back into play, and Liliana slanted her almost colourless, opaque blue eyes at the two women as she said, 'I mustn't keep him waiting; patience has never been one of Zeke's attributes,' in a way that suggested the redhead was only too knowledgeable about the man in question.

'What a truly horrible woman,' Pat murmured as they watched the slim, elegant figure weave her way out of the restaurant. 'She wants a good slap, if you ask me.'

'Probably.' The down-to-earth comment brought a reluctant smile to Marianne's lips. 'But she's incredibly good at what she does and she knows it.'

'I just bet she is.' Pat's sober words had a dual meaning, and the two women stared at each other in perfect understanding for a long moment before Marianne caught the young waiter's eye and gestured that she wanted the bill.

CHAPTER TWO

MARIANNE got back to the apartment at six-thirty and the Mortons were due to arrive at seven. Zeke met her in the cream-and-grey hall, its immaculate walls devoid of any pictures that would deflect from the gracious lines of the curved moulding at the junction of the ceiling and wall, and he was angry. Very angry. As she had expected him to be.

'Where the hell have you been?' he bit out tightly, his mouth a thin line.

'With Pat.' She walked past him towards the bedroom, praying that the trembling in her stomach wouldn't communicate itself in her voice.

She had made some serious decisions this afternoon—somehow seeing Pat again had crystallised so many things in such a short time—and she had to be calm and composed when she discussed them with Zeke. Anything less and he would accuse her of running on nothing but emotion again.

'With Pat.' Zeke was white with rage, his eyes charcoal with the temper he was trying to contain. 'And you didn't think to call and say you'd be late? It didn't occur to you I might be worried something had happened to you?'

'What?' She swung round as she reached the walk-in wardrobe at the far end of the room and her eyes were wide with shock. It hadn't occurred to her he would be worried, she realised with some dismay, merely that he would be angry she wasn't waiting at home with his pre-dinner cocktail ready as usual and a welcoming smile on her lips.

'It didn't, did it?' He had read the answer in her guilty face, and his voice had a harsh, gritty sound. 'Dammit, Marianne, what's the matter with you!'

'Me?' The resolve to remain equable and dispassionate was being put severely to the test.

'Yes, you,' he barked furiously. 'We've got the Mortons arriving any moment and as far as I can see nothing is ready—'

'I couldn't care less about the Mortons!' That was all that concerned him at heart, she told herself silently. He hadn't really been worried about her, just his precious dinner party.

'Obviously.' It was bitingly cold. 'I, on the other hand, do.'

'Of course you do,' she agreed bitterly. 'They come under the heading of ''Work'', don't they? Which takes them into a completely different category to the rest of us poor mortals.' Like Liliana. He needed her expertise for the new project and so the redhead was important to him—far more important than a stay-at-home wife with no career or obvious virtues Buchanan Industries could use.

'Don't be ridiculous.' He strode over to her, whisking back the door of the wardrobe and gesturing violently at the contents as he said, 'Get changed quickly and compose yourself.'

'I'm perfectly composed, thank you very much.' She drew herself up to her full five feet six inches, her voice icy.

'Then get this off and do something with your hair.'

It was his disparaging voice as he glanced at her hair— which admittedly was windswept and tousled from the blustery, cold October evening outside the central heated cocoon of the warm apartment—rather than his hand flicking at her jacket which caught Marianne on the raw.

'Don't do that,' she snapped tightly, her own hand pushing his away. 'Don't touch me.'

'Don't touch you?' He was astounded; it showed in his dark face and the flare of colour across the hard chiselled cheekbones. It was probably the first time the great Zeke Buchanan had ever had that said to him by a woman, Marianne told herself with a touch of silent hysteria. It was certainly the first time *she* had ever said it.

'Yes, don't touch me,' she repeated grimly. 'I'm not one of your possessions, Zeke, whatever you might think. I'm your wife.'

If she had thought he was angry before he was livid now, and as Marianne watched his eyes become coal-black with fury she felt frightened of the demon she had unwittingly unleashed. 'Dead right you're my wife,' he grated slowly. 'So why don't you start acting like it and do what you're damn well told?'

'You arrogant—' As her hand came up to strike him he caught her wrist in one swift movement, and then, without warning, he pulled her abruptly into his arms, crushing her against him as she struggled and fought.

'You're my wife, I'm your husband, so what the hell is this all about?' he ground out savagely. 'What's got into you all of a sudden?'

And then, before she could answer, he had taken her mouth in one of the scorching kisses he did so well, a kiss which immediately ignited a response deep in the core of her.

It had always been like this; he only had to touch her and she melted for him. She had always been defenceless against his expert sensuality, she thought desperately. But she *had* to resist him; she had to make him understand how it was.

'Dammit all, I want you, Marianne.' His voice was a smothered groan against her mouth, his arousal hot and hard against her softness. 'I've been half out of my mind waiting for you.'

Her fingers fluttered helplessly for a second, but then her hands were at the back of his head as she urged his mouth to a deeper penetration, the sensations only he could produce whirling through her body as his lips ravaged the soft sweetness of her inner mouth.

She was moulded into the hard line of his body, her head thrown back against his muscled arm and her body pliant beneath his dominant frame. He was removing his clothes and hers as he laid her on the warm, thick softness of the bedroom carpet, still covering her face with burning kisses, and then they were naked and she could run her hands over the powerful, hair-roughened chest as he bent over her, his eyes wild and glittering.

He continued to kiss and caress her in spite of the hot urgency of need his body was betraying, and piercing pleasure shot through her as his lips moved down her throat and found the rosy tips of her breasts, the nipples hardening into jutting peaks under the ministration of his tongue.

She was more than ready for him when he entered her, her head turning from side to side in an agony of ecstasy and her hair spread out in a glorious silver cascade of silk that shimmered and rippled with their passion.

He held her close to him once it was over, until their pounding heartbeats quietened and steadied, and then he said, glancing at his watch and with a touch of amusement in his voice 'We'd better get dressed unless we want our guests to find us in *flagrante delicto*. And there's still nothing prepared.'

'I've booked a table at that new Italian place John and Katy raved about last week,' Marianne said quietly as she sat up in one fluid movement.

She suddenly felt like crying, and she kept her face turned away as she hurried through to the shower, noticing from the wet towels strewn around that Zeke must have showered when he first came home. For the first time since she had met him she was regretting she had made love with him. They needed to *talk*, everything couldn't always be made right in bed, she told herself feverishly as she allowed the warm water to wash away the feel of his hands and mouth on her hot skin. He had to understand that she couldn't carry on as they were for another day. She was losing sight of who she was and it was terrifying.

'I'll make up a fresh cocktail shaker while you finish getting ready.' Zeke's voice was dark and lazy as he came into the bathroom and talked to her through the glass of the shower cabinet, and for a moment Marianne felt a flood of anger that was all at odds with the image she was going to have to present throughout the evening looming in front of her.

He sounded satisfied, complacent, she told herself tightly—as well he might. He had Liliana drooling over him all day and his wife to satisfy his needs at night—he had it made! She checked the thought in the next moment, recognising it wasn't completely fair. He hadn't forced her tonight, she had met him every inch of the way, so she couldn't very well blame him for her weakness, she admitted miserably. But that was the trouble—she *was* weak where Zeke was concerned. And it had to change—for both their sakes. She would end up hating him if they carried on like this.

She was aware of the Mortons arriving as she sat drying her hair a few minutes later at the dressing table, but she still took her time in getting ready. Zeke's barbed observation about her hair had hit hard, for some reason, probably because she was picturing a sleek, beautifully coiffured auburn head in her mind's eye.

Once her hair was dry she coiled it in a smooth, shining knot on top of her head, before teasing out a few curling tendrils about her face, and then applied her make-up with swift expertise.

The dress she had chosen to wear was a deceptively simple midnight-blue little number, with short sleeves and a high neck, but it fitted her like a glove in all the right places and the colour accentuated her eyes and gave her silver-blonde hair an added lustre. And somehow, for myriad reasons—only a few of which were plain to her—she needed to look her best tonight.

The evening went far better than Marianne had expected on the whole. Gerald Morton she had met before, and thought somewhat arrogant and opinionated, and without realising it she had assumed—erroneously, as it happened—that his wife would be a timid little mouse of a thing. But Wendy Morton was no mouse. She turned out to be a lawyer of some standing, with a manner not unlike Pat's, and her wicked sense of humour added to a tongue that could be acid on occasion kept the conversation fairly buzzing. Marianne found that she liked the older woman very much, and that Gerald actually improved on further acquaintance; not least because she realised he needed to be assertive and confident to avoid being swamped by his feisty wife.

'Gerald tells me you and Zeke have only been married a couple of years.' They had just ordered desserts, and the two men had fallen into the trap of talking business, much to Wendy's obvious disapproval. 'Do you intend to make your home permanently in London?' Wendy asked conversationally. 'You certainly have a super apartment.'

'Thank you.' Marianne hesitated. She could prevaricate or change the subject but everything in her balked at that tonight. 'I don't want to stay in the apartment for very much longer,' she said carefully. 'It was Zeke's bachelor pad before we married and I don't really like it. I'd prefer a house on the outskirts.'

Wendy nodded interestedly. 'Do you work?' she asked mildly.

Zeke was still talking to Gerald, but a sixth sense told Marianne he was listening to the women's conversation, and that more than anything else loosened her tongue. 'Not at the moment,' she said evenly, 'but I intend to look into the possibility of doing a degree course in biology and chemistry with a view to eventually working in a hospital lab.'

'*Really?*' Now Wendy was genuinely interested. 'My sister did exactly that and she's never regretted it. She has done a great deal of work with leukaemic children; you must have a chat with her some time.'

'I'd like that,' said Marianne eagerly. 'Thank you.'

They spoke some more, and although Marianne didn't think Wendy could detect the black waves coming from across the table, she most certainly could.

The desserts were served, and, delicious as Marianne's poached pears with lemon caramel were, she found she had to force them down. She and Zeke were going to have a row—a great, almighty giant of a row—once they were alone; she just knew it. But she had tried, over and over and over in the last months, to tell him how she felt— about the apartment, going to college, the way he kept her wrapped up in cotton wool and separate from the rest of the world—oh, so many things. And he had brushed her aside or treated her like a child who didn't know its own mind. Or both.

She couldn't go on like this any longer, feeling a prisoner in that beautiful, cold, *soulless* glasshouse Liliana had created for him. And he knew how she felt about the elegant redhead, yet he'd still asked Liliana to take on the project, knowing it would involve them working in each other's pockets for days on end.

Her parents' marriage hadn't been like that. Theirs had been an equal partnership, with giving and receiving on both sides; she knew her father had valued her mother's opinion and talked everything over with her. *She wanted to be loved like that.*

She raised her eyes suddenly on the last mouthful of dessert and looked straight across the table at Zeke, and the narrowed grey eyes were waiting for her.

She stared at him, considering him almost as though he were a stranger. He's magnificent! Her brain told her what she really didn't want to hear. She would never, ever meet another Zeke; no man could follow him. It wasn't just the dark good looks, or the brooding magnetism that still had the power to make her weak at the knees, the brilliant force of his personality or the dangerous, almost savage quality to his sensual attractiveness. It was the other side of him, too, the tender, coaxingly soft side that only she saw which in itself made it all the more precious.

He loved her. In his own way he *did* love her, she told herself silently, but whereas he was all her world she was only one small segment of his. She had to decide whether she was prepared to put up with the status quo or insist on change—change that could mean she would lose him altogether. And there was Liliana—and plenty more

Lilianas, no doubt—waiting in the wings should this go against her. She had to remember that.

But she still wanted more than this…this *cage* he'd manufactured around her. If he really loved her he would understand that, wouldn't he?

The waiter arriving with their coffee broke the eye contact and Marianne almost slumped back in her seat before she brought herself up straight. She had to be strong; she couldn't let him intimidate her in any way, this was too important. This situation with Liliana, it had somehow brought to a head everything that had been fermenting under the surface for months.

She had expected Zeke to go for the jugular the moment the taxi dropped the Mortons off at their attractive mews house in Kensington, but after the goodbyes had been said, and they were on their way again he merely settled back in the seat, drawing her arm through his. 'Tired, sweetheart?'

Marianne's reply was lost in his leisurely kiss, a kiss that had her dizzy and flushed and warm by the time he'd finished. She had never met anyone who could kiss like Zeke. She had never met anyone who was such a master of manipulation as Zeke! She took a deep breath and prayed for the right words. 'Zeke, we have to talk. You know that, don't you?'

'I can think of better things to do, but if you insist…' He smiled at her, a slow, sexy smile, and she hoped he couldn't see the effect it had on her. 'Wait till we get home, okay?' he drawled softly. 'We can have a brandy and talk all you want.'

He smelt delicious—Zeke always smelt delicious; it was one of the first things she had noticed about him—and as Marianne rested her head against his broad shoulder she found herself praying she wouldn't capitulate to his charm as she had done so many times in the past. It wasn't that she had set her heart on being a career woman to the exclusion of everything else—she wanted children, Zeke's children, and a family home and slippers in front of the fire; of course she did—but in this day and age it didn't have to be one or the other.

He kissed her again once they were in the lift, and she closed her eyes, her arms snaking up round his wide muscled shoulders and her hands tangling in the spiky short hair at the back of his head. His hands swept over her breasts, her thighs, before coming to rest on her neat rounded buttocks as he urged her against his hard maleness until she could feel every inch of his powerful arousal.

'You're incredible, do you know that?' he murmured against her lips. 'I can never get enough of you.'

The lift slid to a halt and she pushed him away slightly as sanity returned. 'Zeke—'

'I know, I know.' He smiled at her, his eyes crinkling at the corners as his thick short lashes swept down, hiding his expression from her. 'You want to talk first.'

They entered the apartment with his arm round her waist and their bodies touching, but once in the drawing room Marianne purposely seated herself on a blue brocade chair rather than on the sofa, her hands neatly together in her lap and her back straight.

Zeke poured them both a brandy from the gracious cocktail cabinet in one corner of the room, his face faintly amused as he took in her posture.

'Thank you.' Her voice was prim as she accepted the heavy crystal brandy glass from him, and she swilled the dark golden contents around for a moment before taking a small sip.

'So?' He seated himself on the sofa opposite her after taking off his suit jacket and slinging it on a chair, undoing the first few buttons of his shirt and loosening his tie as he settled back comfortably in the seat. 'Talk, my sweet. Talk.'

'My sweet'. It wasn't so very different from 'sweetie', was it? Marianne thought, Liliana's condescending manner in the forefront of her mind as she stared back into the dark, handsome face opposite her. They both thought she was someone to be patronised in their different ways.

The thought made her voice brittle as she said, 'I can't carry on living as we are, Zeke, you must realise that.'

'Why?' It was cool and even but not aggressive.

'Because I don't like it, for a start,' she said bravely, her determination slightly aided by the Dutch courage she had imbibed throughout the meal.

'This little talk couldn't have something to do with the fact that you've spent most of the day with Pat and most of the evening with an equally formidable woman, could it?' Zeke asked with insufferable pleasantness. 'Both of whom regard men as infinitely lesser beings?'

'No, it couldn't,' she snapped back quickly. 'And they don't, anyway.'

'They do from where I'm standing.'

'Then you must be standing in the wrong place.' Oh, this wasn't going at all as she had planned, Marianne told herself silently as she watched his face darken. 'Look, Zeke—' she took a deep breath and forced her voice down an octave or two '—I'm a grown woman and perfectly able to determine what I think without any help from Pat or Wendy. You must have realised things haven't been good between us for some months now?'

'The hell I have!' he said with controlled grimness.

How selfish men could be. As she looked into the breathtakingly attractive face frowning at her Marianne's heart was thumping at the confrontation. He had effec-

tively ignored her cries for help—both verbal and silent—
for months now, wrapped up in his little empire as always.
He had been quite happy for her to remain isolated and
frustrated as long as his world ticked on as normal. She
had been here in her position as the perfect wife as far as
he was concerned, cooking his dinner, entertaining his
friends and business colleagues, putting his interests before
her own and—because she loved him so much—waiting
patiently for him to start making a few decisions on things
that affected *them*.

Maybe it would have been different if they had had
children? Her heart gave a pang as it always did when she
thought of babies, Zeke's babies. And then again it might
have been worse. Perhaps she had to face the fact that there
was something integrally wrong in this marriage. Anyway,
whatever else, she had been patient long enough.

'Are you still upset because I gave the contract to
Liliana?' Zeke asked now, a softer note in his voice.
'Marianne, I needed the best person for that particular
job—it's very important to me—and Liliana is the best
interior designer around. That's all there is to it.'

No, that wasn't all there was to it, she thought painfully.
Oh, why couldn't he *see*?

'Liliana is just a part of it, that's all,' she said quietly.
'It's much more than that.'

'What, exactly?' He leant forward as he spoke, and even
at this crucial moment her senses leapt at the dark, virile
power that radiated out from him.

'This apartment, for one thing.' She waved her hand to
encompass the beautiful room. 'We were going to look for
a house together once we came back from our honeymoon;
you know that. I've never wanted to live in the middle of
London and you promised me we'd find a family house

on the outskirts somewhere, something that was really ours. But it's always "tomorrow" or "next week".'

'This is ours,' he said quickly, a note of surprise in his voice.

'No, it isn't,' she said steadily. 'It never has been. It's yours, just yours.' With Liliana's spectre forever popping up like the evil genie.

'Okay, we'll look next week if you—' He stopped abruptly as her wide azure eyes forced him to hear what he was saying. He ran a hand through his short black crop of hair in an impatient gesture as he rose irritably, walking across to the cocktail cabinet and pouring himself another stiff brandy. 'Marianne, I'm up to my eyes in this new development, but why don't you start looking and narrow it down to just two or three for us to look at together?' he said evenly as he turned to face her again. 'And if we both like something enough I promise you we'll take it, okay? I accept we should have moved sooner.'

'You do?' She stared at him, hope springing up in her heart. 'And you promise we'll move?'

'I promise.' And then he smiled his rare, sexy smile as he added, 'I even promise you can have the last say; you're going to be there more than me so that's only fair.'

She should have challenged him on that—their home was to be a new beginning, just as important to him as it was to her, besides which when she started working for her degree and went on to a career it was likely she wouldn't be at home any more than Zeke—but with him smiling at her like that after the trauma of the last minutes, when she had thought the altercation was going to turn into an argument of momentous proportions, all she felt was overwhelming relief.

She rose to her feet, flying across the room and into his

arms as she said excitedly, 'Tomorrow! First thing tomorrow I'll start looking! Oh, Zeke!'

And then, as he gathered her into him, his passionate kisses taking them both into a blaze of hungry sexuality where the only thing that mattered was the satiation their lovemaking would bring, nothing else seemed important.

Later, once they had showered and gone to bed—only to love some more before settling down to sleep, entwined in each other's arms—Marianne lay awake for some time after Zeke's steady breathing told her he was asleep. A real home of their own would be a new beginning, and she would make it work, she told herself determinedly; she would. She couldn't live without Zeke, she didn't *want* to live without him, and he had met her halfway over this. That was a portent that they'd be happy…wasn't it?

It took Marianne six weeks of looking, as far away as Reading on the one hand and Watford and Chelmsford on the other, but eventually, in the third week of a bitterly cold November, she came across the house which immediately knocked all the others off her list.

Ironically, considering she had had particulars from umpteen estate agents, it was her father who had put her on to the place. She and Zeke had spent the previous Sunday with him, and when she had mentioned they were looking for a family house—preferably on the outskirts of London somewhere, but with modern motorways distance wasn't *too* much of a problem—Josh Kirby had nodded thoughtfully.

'Funnily enough I might know of somewhere to suit you,' he'd said quietly as he'd carved the enormous Sunday joint. 'Old Wilf Bedlows—you remember him, Annie, came to your wedding?—is retiring early; only chatted to him on the phone the other week. He was the only wealthy one among us at medical school; his parents were consultants, so I understand, and as their only son he inherited the family home when they died. Rather than sell it he moved his family in because it was such a beautiful place. Anyway, the kids are grown up and his wife suffers with bad arthritis so they're leaving England for warmer climates. Portugal, I think, or it might have been Spain.'

'And they want to sell their house?' Marianne had asked somewhat wearily. She felt as though she had been rushing from one end of the country to the other for decades, and Zeke hadn't been very sympathetic when she'd had a grumble the night before. Still, at least they weren't arguing—they didn't see each other enough for that since she'd been house-hunting!

'That's the idea, although Wilf's reluctant to put it on the open market, I think. He was born there and I think he's loath to sell to just anyone. He's very attached to the old place.'

'I'm not just anyone.' She'd suddenly had a good feeling about this.

'No, you're not,' her father had agreed with warm smile. 'I'll give Wilf a ring after lunch, if you like, and Zeke can talk to him.'

'*I'll* talk to him,' Marianne had said firmly. 'I'm the one in charge of the house-hunting.'

'Right.' Her father had raised his eyebrows at Zeke, who had shrugged amiably, and then both men had shared an indulgent, male bonding type of smile. Marianne hadn't minded; she was determined to find a house and then start on the next phase of her life, and if it could be done pleasantly all well and good. The iron fist in a velvet glove approach had its uses.

Wilf Bedlows' Victorian white-washed house over-looked a leafy common on the London side of

Hertfordshire, and when Marianne arrived to look at the property on a frosty November morning the weak sun was making the frost glitter like diamond dust on the bare trees and frozen grass.

She sat for some time in the warm, comfortable BMW Zeke had bought for her when they had first got married, just looking at the large sprawling house from her vantage point on the quiet country road running parallel with the common. She loved it already.

Wilf and his wife made her very welcome, and their passion for their home was plain from the beginning, each room reflecting the love and enthusiasm they had poured into the property.

When Marianne entered the large, sloping-roofed porch an immediate feeling of peace and tranquillity surrounded her; the two white Lloyd Loom chairs and small cane table suggested the porch would be a delightful suntrap in the summer.

The hall was impressive: mellow tones of ancient oak dominated the vast space, the staircase, doors and wooden floor all reminiscent of another era. And so it continued all through her tour of the house.

Each of the five bedrooms had its own *en suite* bathroom, the master bedroom overlooking the two acres of ground at the back of the property which were set with informal flowerbeds, flowering bushes and mature trees. Elegant lawns meandered down to the site of a small, exquisitely restored little chapel, surrounded by a bower of roses which Wilf's wife assured her made a sweet-smelling retreat in the summer months.

The large drawing room, family sitting room, dining room and breakfast room were all enchanting, and the big kitchen—complete with bunches of dried flowers and baskets hanging from the walls and ceiling, which gave the red-tiled surroundings a distinctly Mediterranean feel—had a gallery above it which had been enclosed to make a large, sun-filled study.

It was a family house—warm, vibrant, alive and welcoming—and by the time she left after a delicious lunch Marianne had arranged to bring Zeke down to view that same evening.

She hardly knew what to do with herself on the drive back to the apartment, her heart singing and her mind full of colour schemes and new furnishings. Pale green and a warm, buttery yellow for the drawing room—she had always loathed Zeke's icy blue and gold—and the sitting room would have a floral theme, with its French windows opening on to the garden. The kitchen—the kitchen would remain exactly as it was. She *loved* the kitchen. She loved all the house! Oh, she was so *happy*.

She called Zeke's office as soon as she got to the apartment, but Sandra, his very able middle-aged secretary, was apologetic. 'He's had to fly up to Stoke again, Mrs Buchanan,' she said quietly. 'It all happened rather suddenly, a little while ago. He did try to call you but you'd already left Hertfordshire and he couldn't contact you on your mobile.'

'I forgot to take it with me,' Marianne said flatly, feeling a slight sense of anticlimax before she told herself not to be silly. If they couldn't go to see the house together this evening they'd go tomorrow; it really wasn't a big deal. And he might be back in time anyway. Zeke had his own helicopter which he used for short trips like this one; he was forever nipping here, there and everywhere. It went with the territory.

Zeke phoned at six o'clock and he sounded harassed. 'I'm not going to be able to make it back tonight,' he said through what sounded like a babble of voices at the other end. 'There's still a long way to go before we clinch the deal. I'm sorry, Marianne.'

'It's okay.' She bit back the disappointment and made her voice bright as she said, 'The house was wonderful, Zeke. It's the one; I'm sure of it.'

'The house?' And then immediately, 'Oh, yes, of course, the Bedlows place. You liked it, then?'

'I love it,' she said a little flatly.

'Good.' The noise rose in a wave and then died down, and it was in that moment Marianne heard a familiar voice say, 'Zeke? Are you coming, darling? I'm *famished*,' before the babble began again.

Liliana. Marianne stood, the phone pressed to her ear and her body frozen, and stared straight ahead across the room. Liliana was there with him.

'Look, it's chaotic now. I'll phone you later, when we get back from the restaurant.'

She heard Zeke's voice but the power to respond was just not there. 'We'. He'd said *we*. Him and Liliana.

'Marianne?'

She barely knew what she was doing when she replaced the receiver, but then in the next instant she had whipped it up again, lying it down beside the phone with numb fingers.

Liliana was in Stoke with him. He had taken Liliana with him. After all she had said to him about how she felt about the other woman he had chosen, deliberately, to take Liliana with him on this trip. And now they were staying overnight.

She began to pace back and forth, her mind spinning. Had she made a mistake? It was possible. It *was* possible. She was clutching at straws and she knew it. Perhaps her mind had played a trick on her. You heard of such things. He wouldn't have taken Liliana with him; there was no need. The project he had employed the redhead for had nothing to do with the development in Stoke. She must have made a mistake.

She glanced at the address book at the side of the telephone and then picked it up slowly. She shouldn't do this; she *really* shouldn't do this, she told herself sickly as she found Sandra's home number. She should wait until Zeke came home and then ask him calmly and coolly; that was what she should do. But the way she was feeling right now she'd be a gibbering idiot by tomorrow night.

She dialled the number.

'Hallo, Amy Jenkins speaking.'

'Hi, Amy,' Marianne said carefully to Sandra's twelve-year-old daughter. 'Is your mother there? It's Marianne Buchanan.'

'Just a minute and I'll get her.'

Marianne's heart was thudding so hard she was pressing her hand to her breastbone when Sandra's concerned voice came on the line. 'Mrs Buchanan? Is anything wrong?'

'I'm sorry to bother you at home,' Marianne said evenly, 'but I've found a financial file regarding the Stoke project which Zeke has left here. Knowing Zeke it's probably because he doesn't need it, but I wondered if the financial guys have gone with him anyway?' She was safe in this; Zeke *had* left the file in his study, but she knew he had extracted relevant data the night before because she had brought him a cup of coffee just in time to hear him muttering about 'the useless amount of rubbish cluttering up this file!'

'Don't worry, Mrs Buchanan, I'm sure it's all right,' Sandra said soothingly. 'We'd have heard by now if he needed anything.'

'Did any of the financial team go with him?' Marianne pressed quietly. And then she took a gamble that made her shut her eyes tightly as she said, 'Although I suppose there wasn't a lot of room with Miss de Giraud going, too.'

'Oh, there would have been room, but Mr Green had gone the day before,' Sandra explained helpfully. 'I think Mr Buchanan expected that everything would run smoothly and the solicitors could iron out any little hiccups between them, but of course it hasn't turned out like that.'

'No, it appears not.' *Talk naturally. Be upbeat.* 'Not to worry, then, if Mr Green's there. I hope you didn't mind me calling?'

'Of course not, Mrs Buchanan. How's the house-hunting going?' Sandra asked cheerfully. 'Seen anything you like yet?'

They talked briefly for another minute, and then, after thanking Sandra again, Marianne finished the call. But again she placed the receiver next to the telephone. If Zeke rang back she didn't want to talk to him; she didn't even want to hear his voice.

She sank down on to the thick carpet as her trembling legs gave way and remained there for some minutes, in too much agony to even cry, her face as white as lint but her eyes burningly dry.

What was she going to do? She swayed back and forth, her arms crossed and her hands gripping her waist. This was the sort of thing that happened to other couples, not them.

After what seemed like a lifetime, but in reality was only fifteen minutes, she made herself rise, and walked into the kitchen slowly like an old, old woman and switched on the coffee percolator.

She drank two cups of black coffee scalding hot, holding the fine china between her chilled hands as she sought warmth like a small hurt animal. Her mind had gone blissfully numb, overwhelmed by the enormity of the catastrophe, and she sat for another half an hour in a dull stupor.

It was when she walked back into the breakfast room—she rarely used the drawing room by choice, finding its cool perfection chilling—and saw the table covered with her sketches of colour schemes and ideas for the house, that she remembered the provisional appointment for that evening.

She rang Wilf at once, forcing herself to think of nothing but the immediate conversation, and explained in a surprisingly normal voice that Zeke had been called away on business unexpectedly and she wasn't sure how long it would be before he came home, adding she would be in touch within a few days, if that was all right?

Of course it was all right, Wilf assured her brightly. The house wasn't going anywhere, he added before saying goodbye.

No, but she was.

She stared at the telephone as though it had been the one to make the decision, and then nearly jumped out of her skin when it rang shrilly, reminding her she had forgotten to leave it off the hook. She let the answer-machine cut in, her heart pounding so hard she felt faint, and then her brow wrinkled when a heavily accented male voice said, 'Mrs Buchanan? Mrs Marianne Buchanan? It is very important that I speak with you.'

She hesitated, her hand going out to the receiver and freezing. And then she ignored all her finer instincts and picked it up.

'This is Mrs Buchanan,' she said quietly as she turned the machine off. It could so easily have been Zeke's voice, and that would have been the last straw.

'You don't know me, Mrs Buchanan, but I have been seeing Liliana,' the somewhat oily voice said smoothly.

'Liliana de Giraud. Are you aware that she is having an affair with your husband?'

'Yes.'

'Oh.' The baldness of her reply seemed to flummox him for a moment, and then he said, more hesitantly now, 'I was supposed to see Liliana tonight, but she has informed me our relationship is over and that she is at present at a hotel in Stoke with your husband. I thought you should know.'

'Thank you,' Marianne said evenly, forcing down the flood of nausea at hearing it stated so bluntly. 'Goodnight.'

He was speaking again when she put the telephone down on his voice, and this time she remembered to pick the receiver up and lay it on the small occasional table before she left the room.

She only packed an overnight case with the minimum of requirements: her make-up, a change of underwear and a jumper and skirt, toiletries and one or two other belongings. She didn't want to take anything Zeke had bought her but she couldn't exactly walk out naked, she thought with a touch of silent hysteria.

Once that was done she walked across to the dressing table and wrote a short note on the expensive linen notepaper which had been a Christmas present from an old aunt. It was succinct in the extreme.

You have made your choice and I don't ever want to see you again. I'm sure our solicitors can sort out the legal niceties, but as far as I'm concerned our marriage is over right now. Marianne.

She folded the paper over and wrote Zeke's name on it before propping it against the dressing table mirror, where he would be sure to see it as soon as he walked into the room.

And then she pulled on her coat, picked up the case and her handbag and walked out into the hall, where she stared around her a trifle bewilderedly before walking to the front door. But this time she didn't look back.

CHAPTER THREE

THIS really was a case of from the sublime to the ridiculous! In spite of the circumstances there was a thread of dark amusement in the thought as Marianne glanced around the dingy bedsit in Hackney.

When she had left the apartment the night before she had checked into a small hotel a few blocks away, knowing she couldn't walk the streets all night. Beyond that she hadn't been thinking at all; she couldn't—it hurt too much.

She had gone straight to bed and amazingly slept all night, waking early in the morning to driving icy rain against the windowpane and with no knowledge of where she was for a disturbing moment or two. And then she had remembered.

She had burrowed into the comfortable hotel bed for some minutes, finding the hours of deep, restful sleep had cleared her mind and brought some sort of clarity to the situation.

She didn't want to bring anything with her out of this marriage; Zeke could keep his money, the car he had bought her, the jewellery, everything. No doubt people would say she was mad but she didn't care; she didn't want a thing from him. However, that presented immediate problems. Not the least being how she was going to live and eat until she sorted herself out and decided what she was going to do with the rest of her life. A life without Zeke.

She had cried then, for over an hour, until she'd made herself physically sick and told herself enough was enough. She had showered in the small, neat *en suite* bathroom, got dressed, brushed her hair and then called her father.

He had answered immediately and she'd been able to tell he was frantic. 'Annie, thank God! Oh, thank God,' he'd said brokenly. 'Where have you been? Zeke's out of his mind.'

'Zeke? Zeke's been in touch with you?'

'Of course he has. What do you expect when you disappear like that? He's here now—'

And then there had been the briefest of pauses before a familiar male voice had said huskily, 'Marianne? Where are you?'

She'd almost dropped the phone, her heart jumping up into her throat where it had set her whole being pounding as panic flooded every nerve and sinew. She hadn't been able to speak, hadn't even been able to breathe such had been her shock.

'Marianne, are you there? Talk to me,' he'd said thickly. 'I've been thinking all sorts of things since I came back last night and found that note. What's happened to make you behave like this?'

What's happened? The fury at his duplicity had burnt up the weakness the shock had caused in a moment and put acid in her voice as she'd spat, 'Liliana de Giraud has happened, Zeke! Remember her? Your little playmate down in Stoke?'

There had been a moment of silence and then he'd said quickly, 'I can explain.'

'I don't want you to explain, Zeke. I just want you out of my life,' she'd said hotly.

'You don't mean that,' he'd said tersely. 'You're hysterical.'

'No, I'm not hysterical,' she had said, more calmly. 'For

the first time in months I'm thinking clearly, as it happens.' She'd taken a deep breath and stated quietly, 'I want a divorce.'

'Over my dead body.'

'The way I'm feeling right now I'll willingly arrange that,' she'd snapped back before she even thought about it.

It had shocked him, she knew it had shocked him, because his voice had actually been verging on soothing when he'd said, 'Tell me where you are and I'll come and collect you, then we can talk.'

'The time for talking is over,' she'd said sadly. 'Don't you understand even that? Can you deny you took Liliana with you to Stoke and she stayed at your hotel with you?'

'I took her to Stoke, yes, and she did stay at the hotel, but not with me in the sense you mean.'

'I'm not a fool, so don't treat me like one,' she'd said tightly as a new flare of anger had brought every muscle tensing. 'You were with her last night.'

'Last night I was searching the streets and ringing everyone we know to find out where you were,' he'd bitten out forcefully.

'You came back to London?' she'd asked confusedly. 'Why?'

'Why do you think?' Normally the furious, grim tone of his voice would have intimidated her, but not today. Today she hadn't cared how mad he got. 'When we got cut off I tried to ring you back and the phone was constantly engaged. I knew something was wrong. I didn't know if someone had broken in, whether you'd had an accident, banged your head—anything. And so I jumped in a taxi and came home.'

How very noble. 'That must have ruined Liliana's plans for the evening,' Marianne had said cuttingly.

'Hell, Marianne, *listen*! Liliana came up to Stoke with me because she'd got some business there, that's all. You're paranoid about her.'

'Put my father on.'

'What?'

'Put my father on,' she'd screamed furiously.

'Not till I finish talking to you.'

She had put the phone down on him, she remembered now as she walked across to the small grimy window and looked out into the rainy street below, and nothing had given her so much pleasure for years.

Then, in case he tried to trace the call, she had gathered her things together and gone quickly down to Reception to pay the bill; she had been out of the hotel in minutes, only to find the gloomy wet morning was not conducive to walking the streets of London.

After boarding a bus without having the slightest idea of where it was going she had found herself in Hackney, and, having spied a small café, she had bought herself a breakfast she couldn't eat. But in the café's steamy window there had been cards advertising all manner of things, one of them being a bedsit a few streets away above a charity shop.

Thirty minutes later and here she was.

She turned from the window and surveyed the dismal room again. It held a two-seater sofa which converted to a bed of sorts, a tiny table and two somewhat battered straight-backed chairs, and a small single wardrobe, all of which stood on a large square of faded carpet.

One corner of the room was sectioned off by a free-standing, dilapidated bamboo screen, behind which stood an old gas stove, an ancient square sink, two feet of work-top with a cracked bin underneath and a rickety old mustard-yellow six-foot cupboard, containing odds and ends of crockery and kitchen utensils, a kettle and two saucepans, with shelves below for storage of tins and suchlike.

But it was cheap by London standards and that was the main thing, Marianne told herself bracingly, as she walked across and turned on the small spluttering gas fire on the wall in front of the sofa. She still had an old bank account in her maiden name she had never bothered to close after she had married Zeke and which contained a few hundred pounds, but other than that she was virtually destitute.

Of course she could go back to live with her father, but somehow, after being a married woman and living her own life for two years, that was not an option she would consider. Besides which, this way she was truly independent and Zeke didn't know where she was. Which suited her just fine.

The lump in her throat threatened to choke her, and she blinked furiously. No more crying, not now; that could come later, in the still of the night. For now she had to see about finding work—any work: waitressing, retail sales, whatever. She needed something to tide her over the next few weeks while she licked her wounds and decided how best to proceed.

She could do this; she *could*. She wasn't going to crumple; she wouldn't give Zeke and Liliana the satisfaction. Zeke and Liliana… Just coupling their names together in her head made her feel sick, and she took several deep, steadying breaths before turning off the fire in preparation for going out.

Essential groceries and hunting for work—they were the only things to concentrate on at the moment, she told herself firmly. Thinking of Zeke made her feel weak when she needed to be strong, so she wouldn't think of him.

*   *   *

That resolve was sorely tested over the next two weeks.

Marianne had found work almost immediately in a small family supermarket at the end of the street in which her bedsit was situated.

The supermarket seemed to be run on the lines of a corner shop, with everyone who entered it being greeted as an old friend by the Polish family who owned it, and much gossiping and setting the world to rights being done over the fresh fruit and cold meat counters.

On Marianne's first visit on the day she'd arrived at the bedsit the matriarch of the family had winkled out of her that she'd just moved in to number seventeen and was looking for work, and the next day, when Marianne had called in for a pint of milk and admitted she'd found nothing, Mrs Polinkski had offered her a temporary job in the supermarket for a few weeks while her married daughter was away visiting her husband's family in Poland.

Marianne had accepted gratefully; buying a few modestly priced clothes and items of underwear to supplement the basic survival amount she'd left with, plus the first month's rent for the bedsit and setting up with groceries and so on, had eaten into the bank account alarmingly.

The Polinkskis were kind and friendly, and the work was not difficult, but the first two or three days had been a nightmare Marianne wouldn't have wished on her worst enemy. Every moment, whatever she was doing, there had been a separate part of her mind that was mourning and grieving for what had gone.

Part of her hated Zeke and another part ached for him so much it was a physical pain, but on the Sunday morning—her day off from the supermarket, which had occurred three days after she had started work—she'd awoken and realised the whole day stretched before her and she was alone. It had felt so alien, being alone. Not having had a period of self-sufficiency and independence at university, she had gone straight from caring for her father in the family home into a marriage with Zeke, and again she had been giving incessantly.

Suddenly the only person she had to care about was herself. There was no one to look after, no one to share with and cook for, just…her. Marianne Buchanan. And she didn't even have a TV to serve as an opiate against the constant longing for Zeke.

She'd sat up in bed as that thought hit, furious with herself. Wouldn't Zeke just love it if he thought she was mopey and miserable! Well, she wasn't—she wouldn't let herself be.

She had forced herself to get dressed and eat some breakfast and then she had cleaned the bedsit from top to bottom, which had taken most of the day. She didn't think it had ever been really cleaned since the house had been converted to the charity shop, with the bedsit and a storage area for the shop's excess stock—plus a small bathroom—above.

When she had finished the bedsit was squeaky clean and sanitary and she'd been exhausted, but she had made herself go to the cinema while the curtains dried in front of the gas fire; when she'd got home she'd put them up again—hoping the creases would drop out by themselves—and then had fallen into bed and was asleep as soon as her head touched the pillow.

She had written to her father the first evening at the bedsit—just a short note, telling him not to worry and that she was fine, but giving no address—and on the Monday evening she'd written a longer letter, which had been reassuring and warm, but she still hadn't disclosed her whereabouts.

She wasn't quite sure how she had come by the knowledge, but she was certain in her own mind that her father's sympathies were more with Zeke than his daughter, and she found she didn't trust her father not to give Zeke the address if he asked. It would be well meant, she had no doubt about that, but disastrous as far as she was concerned, and she couldn't risk it. In a week or two, when she was thinking straighter, she would contact Zeke herself with regard to the divorce, but for now just getting through each day was enough.

But she was managing—she was coping well, she assured herself as she walked home to the bedsit at the end of her second week of working for the Polinskis. She still had a great lead weight where her heart should be but she wasn't crying herself to sleep every night now, so that was an improvement overall. Definitely. And in spite of her misery one thing had clarified in her mind. She was going to go to university and get that degree she'd put on hold.

She was a survivor. Before the breakdown of her marriage she would never have termed herself such, but she *was* a survivor, all right. Zeke, Liliana, life—she wasn't going to let it all beat her. As long as she didn't see Zeke she'd get through this.

'Marianne?'

She froze, the shock all the more drenching because of the nature of her thoughts. For a wild, desperate moment she hoped the big dark figure that had just stepped out of the shop doorway was a figment of her fevered imagination, but then Zeke took a step towards her, and with an instinct that was pure self-preservation she turned and ran.

He caught her before she had even reached the end of the street—as he'd been bound to. At six foot two and with the physique and fitness of a honed athlete it had been a foregone conclusion, she thought despairingly, as his hand on her arm swung her round to face him and almost lifted her off her feet in the process.

'What the hell did you take off for like that?' he snarled furiously. 'What sort of a monster do you think I am? I'm not going to hurt you, Marianne.'

Not going to hurt her? For a second she almost laughed in his face. He was *killing* her, couldn't he see that?

'How...how did you find me?' she asked shakily, trying to shake his hands off her arms but to no avail.

'Does it matter?' he asked irritably, and then as she continued to stare up into his dark face he added in a quieter tone, 'I hired someone to track you down, if you want to know. Satisfied?'

'You did *what*?' She was more than a little grateful for the outrage that brought her as straight as a ramrod. 'How dare you, Zeke?'

'How dare I?' He swore, very explicitly, which wasn't like him. 'You take off like a bat out of hell, leaving just that note, and you ask me how *I* dare? You're priceless!'

'Just so, and you can't afford me,' she said cuttingly. 'I consider faithfulness of inestimable value and it's clearly just too costly for you.'

He eyed her furiously, the narrowed gaze black with rage. 'I am not going to have this conversation out in the street,' he ground out tightly. 'Okay?'

'Oh, no, no.' As he went to manhandle her along towards the bedsit she resisted in such a way she left him in no doubt she meant business. 'You are not stepping foot into my home.'

'Your *what*?' He stared at her as though she was mad, and perhaps she was, she thought almost dispassionately. The world was full of women who turned a blind eye to their husband's little indiscretions, but she wasn't one of them! She loved him—she didn't want to, but she did love him—and she hated him at the same time, and in finishing their marriage she was losing more than just a beautiful home and a fabulous lifestyle. Those things didn't matter at all. But Zeke; Zeke mattered—not that she could let him see that now.

'My home,' she repeated icily, willing the trembling that had started in her stomach and was threatening to shake every limb not to come through in her voice. 'It might not be up to your lofty standards but my little bedsit is more of a home to me than your empty shell of a place has ever been. I loathe your apartment, Zeke; it's cold and false and worthless.' Just like the woman who had stage-managed it.

'Great.' It was scathingly sarcastic. 'Well, now we've established just how you see my taste—or lack of it— where do you suggest we talk? Because we *are* going to talk, Marianne, even if I have to carry you somewhere kicking and screaming.'

'That won't be necessary,' she said with as much dignity as she could muster, silently admitting to herself that the raw December night *was* bitterly cold, with a nasty north wind that cut the air like a knife. 'There's a little wine bar in the next street that's supposed to be quite nice; we can talk in there.'

'Sure there's enough folk in there this time of night to provide the protection you so obviously feel you need?' he asked caustically.

'Quite sure.' She stepped back a pace and this time he made no effort to restrain her, letting go of her arms as he surveyed her through dark narrowed eyes.

He looked gorgeous. She didn't want to acknowledge that his magnetic attractiveness was as powerful as it had ever been but there was nothing she could do about it. The big charcoal-grey overcoat he was wearing gave his already broad shoulders even more width than normal, and his raven-black hair and chiselled cheekbones turned his face into a picture of angled shadows in the dim light.

Marianne turned sharply, walking back the way she had just run as Zeke fell into step beside her, and she wasn't even aware of the moment they passed the bedsit as she desperately tried to damp down the fierce, searing fire inside her that his presence had produced.

He had come to find her. He had cared enough to instigate a search for her. And then she called on the clear, hard voice of logic to combat the weakness he'd induced. She was his property; that was how he saw it, she told herself savagely. She fitted into his life in the same way as his cars and businesses and other possessions, but she was slotted in under a label entitled 'Wife'.

All this wasn't just about Liliana—bad as that was. How often had she tried to talk to him over the last twelve months in particular, only to be brushed aside or, worse, patronised? He had expected her to be happy just waiting for his return home each evening to the brittle palace he'd installed her in. He was to be her everything; nothing else was supposed to exist for her. *She was glad now they hadn't had children.*

The thought shocked her, causing her to glance up from under her thick eyelashes at the grim, handsome profile as they walked towards the wine bar.

Every time she had had her period she had thought it was the end of the world for a while; she had been so desperately eager to have a part of him growing inside her, filling her belly with their love. But it would have been wrong, very wrong. All that would have happened was that another label would have been attached to her—'Mother of his children'. Wife and mother of his children. And the real Marianne, the Marianne that had died a little more with each month of their marriage, would have been buried so deep she would never have clawed her way out of the abyss. And yet he had loved the real Marianne at first…hadn't he? She wasn't sure about even that now.

Oh, Zeke, Zeke. She found she was crying inside, although her eyes were dry. How had they come to this?

'Are you eating properly?'

'What?'

His deep voice brought her out of the dark morass of her thoughts, and now he repeated gruffly, as he glanced down at her white fragile face, 'I said, are you eating properly? You look thinner.'

Now he mentioned it there were signs of strain about *his* eyes and mouth, Marianne thought suddenly as she wrenched her gaze away from his, and the skin was drawn tight over his cheekbones. 'I'm eating enough,' she said flatly, part of her crying out, Don't let him be nice. I can cope with this if he isn't nice.

'This is crazy, Marianne. You know that, don't you?'

'Here's the wine bar,' she said hurriedly, ignoring the fact that he had stopped to face her as she all but ran the few feet to the steps that led down to the cellar bar.

She thought she heard him swear but she wasn't sure, and then she had negotiated the steps and was aware of Zeke just behind her as she entered the arched doorway into warmth and light and noise.

They found a small table for two in a corner of the bustling bar, and Marianne watched Zeke as he walked across to get their drinks. He looked every inch the assured man about town, she thought, aware—with a kind of painful pride that was terribly misplaced in the circumstances—of more than one pair of female eyes following his progress. Assured and vital and strong, with a sort of dark power about him that was dangerously attractive. It had certainly attracted Liliana de Giraud anyway, she reminded herself tensely.

He got served immediately, despite the others already waiting—he was that sort of man—and returned to her with a bottle of red wine and two large glasses. 'I've ordered a table for two in their bistro upstairs,' he said shortly as he sat down beside her. 'In about half an hour.'

'I don't want anything to eat,' she protested quickly.

'Then you can watch me eat, can't you?' He raised his eyes from the wine he was pouring and she was shocked at the piercingly cold light in the grey orbs.

'Look, Zeke, I agreed to have a talk with you, that's all.' Marianne frowned at him, refusing to be intimidated.

He shrugged lazily as he handed her the glass of wine. 'A talk, a glass of wine, a meal—what's the odds?' he drawled with irritating insolence.

'A wife, a mistress on the side? Yes, I get your drift,' Marianne said cuttingly.

'For crying out loud!' The calm contemptuousness vanished and he sat up straight, almost knocking over his glass of wine. 'Liliana is not my mistress. She's temporarily employed by me, that's all, whatever you call it.'

'I call it adultery,' Marianne said as calmly as she could through the swirling of her stomach. 'And so did her ex when he called me the other night.'

'Her ex?' Zeke stared at her, his dark brows drawn together in a ferocious scowl and his mouth one bitter line. 'What are you talking about?'

'I'm talking about the man who phoned me the night you and Liliana were staying at the hotel and told me he'd been dumped,' Marianne shot back angrily. 'He didn't sound too upset by it, but then perhaps he's used to Liliana's little ways. Whatever, he was most informative about her affair with you.'

'There is no affair.' Each word was bit out through clenched teeth.

'I don't believe you.'

The words hung in the air for a moment, stark and naked, and Zeke's face whitened. 'So I'm a liar as well as an adulterer?' he said with deadly softness.

'It would appear so.' She was frightened, terrified, but determined not to show it.

She watched him take a hard deep breath, and then another one, his eyes fixed on hers and a muscle working in his taut jaw, and then he swirled the wine round in his glass, taking a long swallow before he said, his mild voice at odds with the content of the words, 'It's a good job you're a woman, Marianne, because if a man had just accused me of what you have he wouldn't know what had hit him.'

'It wouldn't make it any less a reality,' she said tightly.

'So, you don't trust me.' He settled back in his seat as he spoke, crossing one leg over the other knee as his grey eyes narrowed to pinpoints of charcoal brilliance. 'Do you still love me?'

'What?' She stared at him, utterly taken aback.

'It's a simple enough question, Marianne,' he said evenly. 'I asked you if you loved me.'

'After what you've done?' she said numbly.

'After what you *think* I've done,' he corrected silkily.

'I don't know how you can ask that! I don't know how you've got the bare-faced cheek to even think of asking that!'

'Cut the splutterings of outrage and affronted virtue,' he said with hateful equanimity, 'and just answer the question. Do you love me?'

'I hate you,' she spat back hotly.

The pinpoints were unblinking as they bored with laser-brightness into her soul, searching, probing. For a long moment she really felt as though her innermost self was being stripped bare. And then he blinked, breaking the spell as he said coolly, 'Drink your wine, Marianne.'

'I mean it, Zeke, I hate you.'

'Perhaps.' He leant forward suddenly and she had to force herself not to jerk backwards as his hand came out to cup her small jaw. 'But love and hate are familiar bedfellows and a damn sight more healthy than apathy, my love.'

'I'm not your love,' she said tensely, furious with the way his touch had triggered frissons of deep, secret intensity in the core of her.

'Yes, you are.' It was imperturbable and composed, and utterly at odds with the anger in her voice and her flushed hot cheeks. 'You are mine and you will remain mine, Marianne, so don't let's have any mistake about that. And now you will tell me about this…lover of Liliana's, and exactly what he said to you. *Exactly*, mind.'

'Go to hell!'

'I've been there over the last two weeks and I didn't like it,' he said with a flat, dark evenness that was chilling. 'And someone, *someone*, is going to pay, my sweet, distrustful little wife.'

CHAPTER FOUR

WHEN Marianne awoke the next morning, after a restless night of tossing and turning, she knew she had been dreaming about Zeke.

She couldn't remember the dreams, but she did know they had carried an elusive, erotic flavour that was all to do with the last few minutes she had been with him.

They had eaten in the bistro after all. It had seemed much simpler to do that rather than to engage in a war of words she had no chance of winning. Besides which, Marianne had been more than a little hungry after a hard day working in the supermarket, and the thought of the cheese on toast she'd had planned hadn't exactly filled her with gourmet delight.

Zeke had been pleasant and attentive during the meal, despite her straight face and monosyllabic conversation. However, once they had climbed the narrow steps into the cold street—the moon shedding a thin, hollow light over the dark pavement as clouds scudded hastily past in the winter night—and Zeke had realised she had no intention of returning with him to the apartment it had been a different story.

He had been softly persuasive at first, confident he would get his own way and that she would relent. Then he had tried ordering her to return home, followed by a far less subtle dose of anger at what he saw as her stubbornness. But Marianne had held doggedly to her declaration that she was never setting foot in the apartment again.

'It's over, Zeke.' They had stood in the dark doorway of the shop in front of the side door which was the bedsit's separate entrance, and she'd shivered as she'd spoken. But it had been more to do with what she was saying than the bitter wind blowing down the street. 'I meant it when I said I wanted a divorce.'

'And I meant it when I said I'd never allow it.'

'What you own, you keep?' she'd asked bitterly. 'Is that it?'

'If you like.' For a moment he had stared down at her in angry frustration, and then, without warning, he had pulled her roughly into his arms. His mouth had been urgent and hungry, and immediately he had fired the need in her; it had been sweet, potent, taking control as it always did when he touched her.

She hadn't even struggled. She twisted in the bed, drawing the covers more securely around her as the icy chill of a winter morning without central heating made itself felt. How could she not have struggled, she asked herself bitterly, after all that had happened? After Liliana. But she hadn't.

Zeke, true to form, had taken full advantage of her mesmerised state, moulding her into him until she'd fitted into the hard line of his body as though she had been born to be there.

He had been the master, dominant and sure of himself, demanding subjugation. And why not? she asked herself now as she opened her eyes and stared up at the cracked ceiling. From the first time she had met him he had held her will in the palm of his hand; she had been his, utterly, and he had known it.

But not any more.

She didn't know who had been more surprised—herself or Zeke—when she had wrenched herself out of his hold, her breath coming in harsh, panting gasps and her eyes wild, but she rather thought it might have been Zeke. He had stood there, his handsome face incredulous as she had told him—ordered him—to go.

'You can't just crook your finger and have me come running,' she'd said heatedly. 'Don't you understand, Zeke? Things have changed.'

'So you are seriously saying you want to throw away more than two years of marriage on a whim?' he'd grated furiously.

'A whim?' It had taken every ounce of her control not to strike him. 'Just the fact that you can say that proves I'm right. You don't know me. You don't have a clue what makes me tick or what I'm going through. Our marriage has been nothing but a sham from start to finish.'

She hadn't meant to say the last words but his accusation had been so wounding she had just wanted to hurt him in return. She didn't know if she had hurt him but she did know she had made him blazing mad; it had been there in the icy-cold eyes that had turned into chips of granite and in the furious rigidity of his face, his lips barely moving as he had ground out, 'one more word—one more word and so help me I won't be responsible for my actions.'

She hadn't provided the word; she hadn't dared to do anything but stare at him silently. And when he had turned in one savage movement before striding off down the street she had remained leaning against the door behind which were the stairs leading to the bedsit.

How long she had stood there she didn't know; it had only been when she was chilled to the bone that she had levered herself away from the flaking wood and fetched the door key out of her handbag.

This was really the end. She touched her lips, which

were still bruised and full from his passionate kisses. She wouldn't ever again wake up beside him after a night of ardent, tempestuous lovemaking and find the smoky grey eyes waiting for her, their warmth intimate and sensual. No more erotic, shameless baths and showers together, when they soaped each other's bodies and found new ways to bring each other to a state of quivering arousal. No more delicious Sunday mornings in each other's arms.

He was a devastating, wonderfully inventive lover, capable of producing such piercing pleasure at times that she had thought she would die from it.

But she hadn't died. She threw back the bed covers and quickly slipped into her thick dressing gown, adjusting the bed back into its daytime position as a sofa so that she could turn on the little gas fire and put some warmth into the freezing room. No, she hadn't died, she thought soberly, as she held a match to the gas jets. She had grown up instead. And she would never have believed it could be so agonisingly painful.

When Marianne arrived at the supermarket an hour later it was to find the place in something of a panic. Mrs Polinkski had had an early-morning fall and dislocated her knee, which meant that Marianne and the Polinkskis's two younger daughters—as yet unmarried—were going to be hard pressed.

Mr Polinkski and the son of the family divided their time between the office and the small warehouse at the back of the supermarket, and neither of them would contemplate working in the front of the shop, despite knowing Mrs Polinkski did the work of two women in her bustling, capable way.

Consequently, by the end of the long day Marianne's feet were aching, her head was pounding with the beginning of what felt like a migraine, and when she glanced in the mirror in the little staff cloakroom before leaving the shop she looked as if she had been pulled through a hedge backwards.

Which made it all the more disconcerting when she emerged into the frosty air and almost into Zeke's arms.

'What on earth are you doing here?' It was a despairing cry and he recognised it as such, his mouth—which hadn't been smiling as it was—tightening still more into a hard line.

'Waiting for you,' he bit back grimly. 'And that should have been my line, not yours. I can't believe my wife is killing herself working all hours in a two-bit shop in the back of nowhere. You look terrible.'

'Thank you so much,' she shot back furiously. It was the last thing, the very last thing, she needed to hear.

He made no apology, his face even more belligerent as he scowled ferociously at an inoffensive couple who had been laughing as, arm in arm, they approached them. The laughter stopped and the young couple sidled past, the man putting his arm more protectively round his girlfriend and keeping his eyes warily on Zeke's dark face until they were well clear.

'Your father is in the car.'

'*What?*'

The icy eyes narrowed but his voice was silky as he repeated, with elaborate and insulting patience, 'Your father is in the car.'

'You've brought my father here?' she hissed angrily. 'That's despicable, absolutely despicable, and you know it.'

'"Despicable" is not a word I'd choose when someone is trying to allay another person's worry about the daughter they love,' he said with sickening self-righteousness.

'Oh, isn't it?' She eyed him furiously, her blue eyes

sparking and her face flushed. 'You brought him here so he could add his weight to yours and persuade me to go back to the apartment. Admit it!'

'Not at all,' he said with cool indifference.

'Liar.' He didn't like that, and so she repeated it for good measure before going on to say, 'Have you told him about Liliana?'

'I've told him what you have accused me of and I've also made it plain it's totally without foundation,' Zeke said coldly, his eyes glittering.

'I just bet you have,' she agreed bitterly. 'And of course he believed you.' She had heard Zeke too often in the past not to know he was capable of making anyone believe black was white when he put his mind to it. But not her. Not any more.

'Your father can recognise truth when he hears it, which is another reason he is here tonight,' Zeke said a trifle cryptically.

'What do you mean?' There had been something there she didn't understand. 'If you think you can get my father to induce me to accept what I don't believe, you're wrong, Zeke,' she warned heatedly. 'You'll just upset him, that's all. I love him, very much, but I won't perjure myself for him or you. This is too big for me not to be honest. It's also between you and me,' she added resentfully. 'You had no right to try and use him to get to me. I didn't think even you would stoop so low.'

'You've turned into quite a shrew, haven't you?' he mused thoughtfully, his breath a white cloud in the icy air. 'If this is what living by yourself does in two weeks I'd say it's even more reason to come home.'

'The apartment has never been my home; I've told you that.'

'And you're happy to let the Bedlows' place go?' He

always knew how to go for the jugular. 'Your sketches and colour schemes were spot-on, by the way.'

She wasn't falling for that one, Marianne thought angrily. He could use his charm on someone else! 'Perhaps you should have employed me instead of Liliana?' she suggested with an acid smile. 'It would have saved the company a lot of money and you a lot of trouble in the long run.'

'Perhaps I should have,' he agreed softly.

She stared at him, aware that Zeke was never so dangerous as when he was being inscrutable. Like now. Marianne decided to change the subject. 'Where's the car?'

'Round the next corner.' He smiled a shark smile. 'I thought it only fair to give you a chance to compose yourself before you saw your father.'

'You really do think of everything,' she acknowledged with withering coolness. 'Although you made a little mistake with regard to Stoke. It wasn't quite far enough away to keep everything under wraps, was it?'

'Marianne, if I had been entertaining a mistress, as you seem so determined to believe, I wouldn't have made any mistakes,' he returned smoothly, the street lamp picking up the shining jet of his hair.

She tossed her head, terribly aware of her own bedraggled locks and the fact that she was minus a scrap of make-up, and began to walk with as much dignity as she could muster.

'Ahem.'

She turned back, eyebrows raised enquiringly, to see Zeke looking at her with an expressionless face as he pointed down the street in the opposite direction from which she was walking. 'I don't believe I said which corner,' he said evenly, with a flatness that told her he was trying not to laugh.

Zeke had two cars besides the company car—a Mercedes—and the helicopter which he used frequently, and when Marianne turned the corner she saw it was his white BMW that was waiting patiently a few yards away.

Her father had been sitting in the front seat, but he'd obviously been using the mirrors because he was out of the car in an instant, reaching her in a couple of strides and lifting her off her feet in a bear hug which spoke volumes about how concerned he'd been.

Marianne immediately felt guilty—both on her father's account and also because she realised Zeke had been speaking the truth when he'd said her father needed to see her and make sure she was all right. Not that she didn't think Zeke had an ulterior motive for his altruism, she assured herself silently. Zeke was always playing some game of his own, whatever else he liked people to think. She might not have known her husband as she'd thought she did, but there were certain aspects of his character that were blindingly clear!

'Zeke's taking us out for dinner.'

They had been holding each other very tightly without speaking, and when her father drew back a little and looked into her face she saw his eyes were wet. Which made her feel such a heel that she didn't object to his statement, although she wanted to. What Marianne did say was, 'I'll have to change first and freshen up. It's...it's been a hectic day; someone was ill.'

'No problem.' Zeke had been standing to one side, his smoky grey eyes trained on her face during the reunion, and now his voice was clipped and cool as he said, 'We can wait until you're ready.'

'I won't be long.'

'Hey.' Her father caught hold of her arm as she made to dart away, smiling at her before he tucked it through his, saying, 'Aren't you going to show me where you're living?'

Oh, hell. It was a catch-22 scenario. If she took her father back to the bedsit Zeke would have to come, too, and she didn't want him to see the shabby, run-down conditions in which she was living. But if she refused to let her father accompany her he would be bound to think the conditions were even worse than they were, or that she had something to hide, or— Oh, a host of things. She was between the devil and the deep blue sea.

'Later, perhaps?' She forced a smile. 'It's just a bedsit, Dad. One room, and I need to change.'

'We'll come out and wait in the car while you change.' Zeke actually had the gall to take her other arm as he spoke and now Marianne found herself being escorted along the pavement with the two men either side of her.

Everything in her wanted to jerk her arm free of Zeke's and say something very rude to put him in his place— whatever that was—but, conscious of her father and the emotional greeting he'd given her, she tried to ignore the anger spreading through her and keep any trace of it out of her voice. 'It's not very attractive,' she said quickly as they neared the house, 'but it's cosy and cheap and it will do until I find something better.' She didn't think it was the time to mention that that wouldn't be for years.

Her father glanced at her, and as she met his gentle eyes she read in them that he was aching to advise her to go back to her husband. But, to give him his due, Josh Kirby held his tongue on the matter, merely murmuring, 'I'm sure it's very nice, Annie.'

Zeke said nothing, but his cynical profile—as she risked a quick glance at him from under her lashes—said volumes.

Marianne could feel her heart thudding against her ribcage as she unlocked the street door, and as she led the way up the stairs towards the bedsit's front door there were a thousand emotions tearing at her. But when she inserted the key into the lock and swung the door wide before clicking on the light she raised her head high.

She walked across the room and closed the curtains, which, courtesy of Mrs Polinkski's iron, were now crease-less, and she blessed the fact that a couple of days before she had bought a woven linen throw in burnt orange for the sofa, obtained from the charity shop at a fraction of the price it was worth. Nevertheless, no number of throws or bright clean curtains could disguise the overall mean-ness of the surroundings, and Marianne took a long deep breath before she turned round.

Her father looked shocked—there was no other word for it—and Zeke had his blank face on. Their combined silent censure brought her chin up another notch or two as she faced the two men.

She knew her father wouldn't say anything hurtful but she was preparing herself for one of the biting, caustic comments Zeke did so well. But it didn't come. Instead he slowly met her eyes, and she found the expression in the smoky grey depths brought her hand to her throat as he said quietly, with a vulnerability she hadn't thought him capable of, 'You would rather live here, like this, than have to live with me again.' And it was a statement, not a ques-tion.

She couldn't drag her gaze away from his stricken eyes, although she wanted to, and it was only her father—clear-ing his throat and speaking gruffly into the taut silence—who brought things back to a more normal footing as he said, 'We'll wait in the car, then, Annie.'

'Yes, yes, all right.' She wanted to cry, she wanted to cry *so* much, but she managed to keep a check on her feelings until the door had closed behind them and she was alone. And then the tears came, hot, burning, desolate tears, even as she told herself that she mustn't cry—they would be sure to notice and that would be the final humiliation.

She pulled herself together fairly quickly. She could cry tonight, and all the other nights, but for now she had to get through this evening with a modicum of dignity. What had just happened—it didn't alter the *facts*. He had taken Liliana to Stoke with him; they had been going out to dinner when he had called her. And that man, Liliana's boyfriend, he had been very specific as to the manner of Zeke and Liliana's liaison. And Zeke hadn't been compelled to employ the stunning redhead, especially knowing how Liliana felt about him. It had been asking for trouble, and Zeke Buchanan wasn't a naive teenager who didn't know the ways of the world. He had deliberately chosen to play with fire and it had burnt both of them.

Thoughts were swirling around in her head as she hastily splashed cold water over her face and whipped off her creased work clothes, only to come to an abrupt halt as she opened the wardrobe and surveyed the meagre array of clothes inside.

She had absolutely nothing which was suitable to go out to dinner in. The clothes she had purchased in recent days had been bought purely for their suitability for working at the supermarket, and were functional at best.

Her eyes alighted on the dress she had been wearing when she had left the apartment, a beautiful long-sleeved cashmere in chocolate-brown, and then moved to the jumper and skirt she'd thrown in the overnight case. They were expensive, and they looked it, but they belonged to her old life. She had only kept them because it seemed ridiculous to get rid of them until she'd purchased a few more bits and pieces.

Her hand reached out to the cashmere before falling to her side. Somehow, and she couldn't explain it even to herself, let alone anyone else, it would seem like a betrayal of everything the last miserable, lonely two weeks had stood for if she put on clothes Zeke had bought for her.

She hadn't asked to be taken out to dinner tonight, and if Zeke was ashamed of how she looked then that was his misfortune, she told herself stoutly. She wasn't the long-suffering, obedient little wife any more, who couldn't say boo to a goose, neither was she a sleek, exquisite, designer-dressed Liliana de Giraud.

She had been wearing a pair of old jeans and a skimpy, much washed little top that summer's day when she had first seen Zeke, she remembered flatly. Her hair had been loose in silky disarray and her only jewellery had been large silver hoops in her ears. Where had that carefree, happy-go-lucky girl gone?

She looked again at her wardrobe, and then her mouth lifted slightly at the corners. She knew what she was going to wear now.

The BMW was parked outside the house when Marianne exited ten minutes later, and Zeke leant across from the driver's side and opened the front passenger door for her. She slid into the front seat, turning briefly to smile at her father, and then said calmly—as though her stomach wasn't turning over and over— 'Where are we going to eat?'

'Salamanders,' Zeke said shortly.

Thank you—oh, thank, God, she prayed fervently. She had been worried he was going to say Rochelle's, and the jeans she had bought for weekends and the waist-length bubblegum-pink cardigan—another acquisition from the shop below that she had spied the previous Saturday and leapt on as soon as the shop had opened—were definitely not Rochelle material. Salamanders... Yes, Salamanders encouraged their clientele to be different. She could pass for capricious at Salamanders and it would be to her credit.

Salamanders was *the* restaurant of the moment, and when Zeke drew up outside its relatively innocuous portals and a doorman leapt to take care of the car, she gave a secret nod of acquiescence to the little voice in her head that said, You're back in *his* world now, even if it is only for one evening.

Well, yes, she might be, she agreed silently, but this time she was going to make darn sure it was on her terms.

She had fixed her hair in a cute 60s ponytail on the side of her head, her make-up was discreet but flattering, and as she walked into the restaurant on the arms of her father and her husband she knew she looked good. She might not look like a millionaire businessman's wife, or the latest designer clothes-horse, but she looked good. As *she* wanted to look, like the person she was inside.

Their table was waiting for them—Zeke would have expected nothing less—and as Marianne followed Zeke, her father making up the rear, her eyes suddenly become riveted on the woman the waiter was walking towards. It couldn't be! He wouldn't have! She kept on walking but her mind was screaming a warning. How could he? How *could* he do this? Surely her father hadn't agreed to this?

'Zeke, darling.' As they reached the table Liliana's heavily made-up eyes flicked over Marianne and her father, and Marianne realised the lovely redhead was as taken aback as she was. 'We're going to have a little party! How lovely.'

'I thought so.' Zeke inclined his head towards Liliana's table companion as he turned to Marianne and Josh and said coolly, 'Marianne, you know Liliana, but not her brother, I think? Josh, may I introduce you to Liliana and Claude de Giraud?'

'Good evening.' Josh was nothing if not a gentleman, but Marianne could tell he had recognised the name as the third corner in his daughter's particular little triangle, and also that he didn't appreciate her being put in such a position. The look he bestowed on Zeke was piercing, and it was not amiable.

'Trust me.' Zeke answered the beetling eyebrows quietly, his voice flat but holding a message Marianne didn't understand.

'This had better be good, Zeke.' For once Josh was not his easygoing self. 'I believed you were genuine when you said you had Marianne's best interests at heart.'

Josh's voice was too low for the two sitting at the table to hear, but her father had drawn Marianne to him with a protective arm and she heard every word. She didn't know what to do or think. If her father hadn't been there to give her moral support she had to admit she would have probably turned tail and run—despite the satisfaction that would have given the beautiful redhead. As it was, she forced herself to smile politely and incline her head just the slightest as she said, 'Liliana, Claude, good evening.'

Once they were seated there was a split second of screaming silence before Zeke said, 'A cocktail, I think, before we order?'

Marianne eyed him balefully. If he wasn't too careful he might find one particular cocktail ended up all over his dark, adulterous head, she thought viciously. 'Lovely.' She smiled sweetly. 'I'll have a Pink Slammer, to match my top.'

She had been aware of Liliana's eyes on the jeans and cardigan, and it didn't need an expert in psychology to work out Liliana was doing her sums. Marianne had decided attack was the best defence.

Liliana was dressed to kill in a black slinky number that fitted where it touched, with a hairstyle that must have taken her hairdresser hours. Her brother was equally expensively dressed, his suit clearly handmade and his shirt and tie in raw silk.

'What a darling idea!' Liliana seemed to have recovered her poise, her ice-blue eyes deadly as she allowed her gaze to rest on Marianne's jeans for one moment before she said, with a little tinkling laugh, 'A Black Widow for me, sweetie.'

The waiter was at their elbow taking orders in the next instant, and it was a second or two before he moved away and Liliana said, resting a red-taloned hand on Zeke's arm as the opaque gaze flicked round the table, 'It was just so sweet of you to invite Claude and I along tonight, darling, but what's the occasion?'

'I rather thought you could provide the answer to that, Liliana. You and Claude, of course.' Zeke's voice was silky-soft but Marianne glanced at him sharply. She knew that tone; she'd heard it once before, in the early days of their marriage, when they had been sitting in the garden of a riverside pub and some youths—aged fifteen or sixteen, certainly old enough to know better—had thought it good fun to throw stones at a swan and her signets.

They had been seven to Zeke's one but he hadn't had to swing a punch. The look in his eyes and the tone of his voice had had the bunch of yobbos all but crawling in the dirt in front of him.

Liliana wasn't exactly crawling in the dirt, but she was intelligent enough to know that all was not well. The hand was removed from his arm and she settled back in her chair, glancing round the table once more before she said, 'I don't understand?'

'Now, isn't that strange.' Zeke glanced from her to her brother. 'I thought you might just click on when you saw us come in. And you, Claude? You also do not understand?'

'Zeke…' Claude's voice trailed away, but the one word was enough to make Marianne's eyes open wider. She knew that voice.

'Yes?' Zeke had fixed Claude's eyes with his own and the Frenchman was wilting.

'Zeke, this was not of my doing. You must understand that. I did not want to be a party to it—'

'Shut up!' Liliana's voice was malignant. She said something in French to her brother that was clearly not complimentary.

'Go on.' Zeke hadn't taken his eyes off the Frenchman when his sister had spoken. 'You did not want to be a party to what, exactly?'

'You know what.' Claude had gone ashen. 'I tell her. I tell her that this is not good, that it will end badly. I tell her but she won't listen.'

'Elucidate,' Zeke bit out savagely.

Claude darted a glance to the left and right of him, clearly terrified. 'She wouldn't listen,' he whined nervously. 'She said if I still wanted money I had to do it. She said you would never find out.'

'You made the phone call.' Marianne had half risen in her seat, one hand gripping hold of her father's arm and the other pointing at the big florid Frenchman in front of her. 'You said that you were Liliana's lover, that she was having an affair with Zeke.'

'Of course he did.' Zeke's voice was full of contempt. 'I have known Claude for years, and he does whatever his

sister tells him to do. That is so, isn't it, Liliana? Claude
has a little problem, an expensive little problem, and big
sister provides the cash for his habit in return for his absolute devotion to the cause of promoting Liliana de
Giraud at all times and giving her exactly what she wants.
He would murder his own grandmother if Liliana required
it.'

'A slight exaggeration.' Liliana's head was up and she
was far from beaten.

'I don't think so.' For the first time Zeke glanced the
redhead's way and there was a dangerous glitter in his
eyes. 'You tried to set me up that day when you said you
had an appointment in Stoke, didn't you, Liliana? And no
one—no one—does that to me and gets away with it. By
the time I've finished with you you will be lucky to get a
job anywhere in England, let alone London. But you made
a mistake in using Claude. I keep my ear to the ground
and I knew damn well you hadn't got a lover at that moment; the rest, as they say, is history.'

She had thought Zeke looked at her strangely last night
when she had mentioned Liliana's ex phoning her,
Marianne thought numbly. He had guessed then; she was
sure of it. And so he had organised what the redhead and
her brother had thought was a nice cosy meal for just the
three of them. And that meant... The numbness was beginning to wear off. That meant their affair was purely in
Liliana's dirty little mind.

'I could say we're having an affair anyway.' Liliana's
red-painted mouth was white round the edges with rage
and furious resentment at the position Zeke had placed her
in.

But now it was Josh who spoke, and he sounded very
much the doctor as he said quietly, 'Why humiliate your-

self any further, Miss de Giraud? It seems to me it is not only your brother who needs help.'

'Zeke does love me. He does. We should never have parted; he knows that at heart. I'm far better suited for him than her!'

Marianne didn't wilt beneath the savage enmity of Liliana's eyes as they flashed her way, but inside her spirit shrank at what was almost madness in the other woman's gaze. She was unbalanced, Marianne thought sickly. She had to be.

And then Zeke challenged the thought as he said softly, 'She doesn't need help, Josh, not in the way you mean anyway. She is obsessed, all right, but not with me, not really. Liliana always comes first with Liliana, and when I finished our relationship some years ago she couldn't accept that a man had actually chosen to walk away from her. It was the first time it had happened, you see; before me it had always been Liliana who ended the affairs. She wants what she can't have, like a spoilt child in a toy shop, and when she gets the toys she wants she takes delight in breaking them. I knew that by the time I left her, but she fooled me inasmuch as I thought she'd accepted how things were between us and ceased to care. I'd never have offered her the job otherwise.'

Josh looked straight at Zeke now, as he continued to grip his daughter's hand beneath the table, and said drily, 'It seems to me you shouldn't have offered it to her anyway. Not one of your best decisions, Zeke.'

Zeke looked back into the older man's calm eyes and then nodded slowly. 'No, it wasn't,' he agreed expressionlessly.

Liliana had clearly had enough of being discussed as though she was not present. She rose in one fluid, sinuous movement of black silk and glared at them all as she spat,

'You'll pay for this; you see if you won't. I won't be treated like this.'

'Sit down.' Zeke didn't raise his voice. He didn't have to; he was quite terrifying enough as it was.

Marianne had always known he could be a formidable opponent—he must have been to get from where he'd started to where he was now—but she was seeing the cold, hard side of him in action for the first time and he was frightening.

His eyes were like piercing steel as they skewered Liliana's, and his voice was glacial, penetrating the thought process like liquid ice.

Liliana sat. The devil himself would have sat.

'I can make you wish you were dead, Liliana,' he said, softly but clearly, 'in a hundred different ways you haven't even thought of. I can strip you of your reputation, make sure you never work again, arrange it that you never get invited to another show, another first night, another exclusive party. And I would do it without any compunction after what you've done. You understand that?'

Liliana opened her mouth twice to speak, but all she could manage was a nod of her carefully coiffured head.

'No one touches me and mine, and you give Marianne the respect due to her as my wife when you address her. Okay? She is worth a hundred of you and you know it; that's what really eats you up. The contract is cancelled as from now and you'll get out of London if you know what's good for you. One word, one whisper against me and mine, and I'll make sure you suffer the torments of the damned.'

'Zeke—Zeke, I didn't mean it.'

'Yes, you did, and we both know it. You would have wrecked my marriage on a pack of lies without a grain of truth in them. I don't want to hear that you're back in town for a very long time, Liliana, and just be thankful I'm holding my hand and you can still work in Paris and Milan and New York.'

The waiter chose that moment to arrive with their cocktails, and he placed each one in front of them hurriedly, his antennae picking up that this was not a good time.

Liliana watched him depart and then she picked up the fluted glass of deep, almost black liquid and drained it, replacing it on the table with a flourish that wasn't lost on the rest of them before she rose gracefully to her feet.

She might be a lying, venomous little snake, without a moral to her name, Marianne thought, but one thing was undeniable. Liliana had class.

'Goodbye.' The opaque eyes swept over each one of them as Claude shuffled to his feet beside his sister. 'I will be sure to be in Paris by the end of the week. Will that suffice?' Liliana asked Zeke, her voice cool and even but her cheeks flushed with high, angry colour.

He nodded dismissively and then turned to Josh and Marianne. 'Another cocktail?' he enquired pleasantly. 'And I think we'll have a bottle of Bollinger with our meal…to celebrate.'

There was a moment's silence as Liliana continued to stand there, unable to believe she had been dismissed in such a cursory fashion, and then she swept out of the restaurant with a muttered oath, Claude trailing behind her.

'Whew.' Josh leant back in his seat on a long sigh. 'You sure know how to keep an evening buzzing, Zeke.'

'Are you all right?' Zeke ignored Josh, reaching across to touch Marianne's arm.

She was trying hard to conceal her emotions—she wasn't even sure what half of them were. Relief, overwhelming, blinding relief was there, along with stunned amazement, incredulity, confusion, wonder, shock, and a certain puzzling panic that at the moment was vague and indeterminate. 'Yes, I'm all right,' she said slowly, 'although it's hard to imagine someone that can be so devious.'

'Devious, manipulative, selfish, downright evil...' Zeke included Josh in the turn of his head. 'You're right, Josh. Not one of my best decisions.'

'I'm...I'm sorry, Zeke.' Marianne raised her head and looked directly into the smoky grey eyes as she spoke. 'I should have known you weren't having an affair with her.'

But how should she have known? she asked herself in the next instant, barely aware of Zeke murmuring some soothing reply before Josh engaged him in conversation. Their whirlwind courtship and swift marriage had meant she'd barely been familiar with even the basics of what made Zeke tick when she'd married him. Those few golden weeks had been a haze of romantic dinners and thrilling excursions into London for shows and parties. They had talked of a big house in the country and of filling it with children and cats and dogs, of holidays abroad, the wedding, their honeymoon. But when had they talked about *themselves*, bared their souls and got to *know* each other? They hadn't.

She sat sipping at her frothy pink cocktail, more disturbed than she had ever been.

And when they had come home from their honeymoon—a time spent almost exclusively in bed as the sensuous hunger of their love had obliterated everything else—Zeke had picked up his old life again almost as though he didn't have a wife, and she had found herself imprisoned in a beautiful, cold, empty shell of a home.

The babies hadn't happened and so the house hadn't happened; he hadn't made time for something that wasn't necessary just because she kept asking for it, needing it. When she had talked of finding a job he had been gently dismissive at first—'You don't need to work, darling, and I want to look after you. It's so wonderful to know you're here waiting for me when I come home.' And then the gentleness had faded and he'd become curt, cold, if she expressed a wish to work outside the home. And she, mindful of his childhood and all he'd never had, had fallen in with his demands, wanting to remove all memory of past hurts and slights.

Not that she had been actively unhappy, not at first. They had had a busy social life—all Zeke's friends and business contacts, of course—and had enjoyed their evenings at home together, which had always finished in one way. They were perfectly suited in bed, desire flaming between them if they so much as touched one another.

But after a few months she had become frustrated, bored and restless, and it was then she had felt the pressure from Zeke to change, to conform to what he wanted in a wife. And because she loved him so much she had done just that—which had been bad for both of them, she thought now.

He had changed from the Zeke she had first loved and she had become someone she didn't recognise, losing her confidence, her belief in herself, everything that made her *her*. Zeke hadn't wanted a real wife—he'd demanded a pretty little doll he could dress up and keep in an elegant doll's house. And she'd fallen in line.

'Marianne?' The waiter was in front of her, holding out an embossed menu as Zeke's voice carefully prodded her back into the present. 'How about caviare to begin with? You enjoy the way they do it here.'

She glanced at him, seeing the dark good looks, the quiet, controlled arrogance and the devastatingly magnetic sexual attraction, and her stomach turned right over. She loved this man, and she was probably going to lose him altogether, but she couldn't go back to the way things had been. She couldn't follow him mindlessly through life; she had her own goals to aim for and dreams to realise. She was a person as well as a wife, and if she had to choose between Zeke or losing her identity...

'No, I don't really like caviare, Zeke,' she said clearly. 'I don't think I ever have. I just tried to, for you.'

'For me?' He stared at her, puzzled but still smiling, and she nearly chickened out. Nearly.

'Yes, for you,' she said quietly. 'But it's probably just as well I don't care for it because I certainly won't be able to afford it in the future, on a student's budget.' Then she raised her eyes to the young waiter as she said, 'I'll have the Parmesan and bacon salad, please, followed by the salmon in lemon and white wine.' And as the ponytail dipped and dived about her hot cheeks she finished the last of the pink cocktail.

CHAPTER FIVE

WHEN Marianne awoke the next morning the room was filled with a strange light hue and it was quiet, very quiet. Unusually quiet. She glanced at the monstrous plastic wall clock some previous occupant had fixed on the wall over the fire. Six o'clock. Early, but not so early that the hum of London traffic shouldn't be making itself known in the background.

She stuck her nose out of the covers and took a deep breath before diving for her dressing gown. Having lived with central heating all her life she couldn't believe how cold the room got during the night.

'Oh, gorgeous…' When she pulled back the curtains the thick, white, starry flakes of snow falling from a laden sky brought her eyes opening wide. It had been ages since it snowed; the last two years they hadn't seen any in London, and it was so *beautiful*.

For a moment she forgot all her troubles and remained staring out of the window like a child spying its presents on Christmas morning.

The dismal street had been transformed into a winter wonderland, ethereal and pure and white, and the snow was already several inches thick. She could see parked cars, like huge rectangular snowballs, completely covered by the feathery mass, and halfway down the street someone was already beginning to clear their vehicle preparatory to beginning the day.

As she watched, a family saloon came down the street,

very slowly, before disappearing round the far corner and leaving deep indentations in the snow.

Thank goodness she hadn't got to rely on a car or public transport to get to work. It was going to be chaotic on the roads this morning. She felt a brief glow of pleasure at her autonomy before she shivered convulsively and set to work restoring the bed back into a sofa. Soon the gas fire was blazing away, she had a steaming cup of coffee at her elbow, and she was snuggled on the sofa with her duvet wrapped around her as she sipped at the drink.

Would Zeke be awake yet? Suddenly all the brief magic was gone. He had been angry last night, furiously angry, and when he had seen her home, after they had taken her father to pick up his car from the apartment car park where he'd left it, the atmosphere had been tense and electric.

She had thought, once they were alone, that he would allude to her comment about becoming a student, but he hadn't, and when she had tried to broach the matter he had been curt and hostile in his refusal to discuss it.

Perhaps she shouldn't have pushed it at that point? she asked herself as she placed the empty coffee cup on the floor before pulling the duvet's thick folds more securely round her. The evening had been one of highly charged emotion as it was, and he'd obviously clicked on to the fact that she wasn't going to fall into his arms and go home with him, in spite of what had come to light regarding Liliana.

But when they had reached the bedsit and she'd become aware he intended to drive away without another word something had snapped. She'd screamed at him, she reflected miserably, positively screamed. 'How can you say goodnight like that and just leave?' she'd shouted. 'What's the matter with you anyway?'

'Me?' There had been savagery in his eyes as he'd

swung round to face her in the car. 'I said goodnight because it is perfectly obvious you don't want to be in my company a second more than is necessary, that's all.'

'That is not all.'

'Oh, yes, it is, Marianne. You heard Liliana and Claude, you know there's nothing between Liliana and I, but you don't want to come home. End of story.'

'End of story?' She hadn't been shouting then; her voice had been scarcely a whisper. 'We haven't talked anything out, Zeke,' she'd said brokenly, 'so how can it be end of story? This is our marriage you're talking about. *Our marriage.*'

'You think I don't know that?' he'd said in cold, clipped tones.

'I've no idea what you know or don't know,' she'd said grimly. 'How could I have? You never talk to me, not really, and you never listen either. Everything, *everything*, is on your terms, always. I'm expected to sit at home twiddling my thumbs all day and wait for you to return from the world of million-dollar deals and fast living, and then just be the sweet, docile wife with the dinner ready and the bedclothes laid back.'

'Don't be ridiculous,' he'd said harshly. 'It's not like that.'

'It's exactly like that.' She glanced at him, but he'd been staring ahead, his features rigid. 'I know I shouldn't have believed you were having an affair, but everything pointed to it, don't you see? Liliana is in your world, and she's vibrant and alive and interesting. And you needed her, needed her expertise and flair. Certainly more than you needed me,' she'd added bitterly.

'What?' His eyes had flashed to her for a moment. 'You can't believe that.'

'Well, I do.' She'd taken a deep breath. 'I've become

someone else since I married you and I don't like it; I
don't like *her*, the person I see in the mirror every morning. You wouldn't talk about my getting a job or doing
voluntary work. You didn't like it if I saw Pat or any of
my old friends. I've been in a strange sort of limbo and I
can't take it any more.'

'So you're walking out on me,' he'd said brusquely, his
face looking as though it was carved in stone.

'I want…I want time—time to think,' she'd said painfully, her heart thudding. She'd been able to smell the delicious scent of him, a mixture of expensive aftershave and
musky male skin, and every fibre of her being had wanted
to throw herself into his arms and agree to anything he
wanted. But she couldn't, not now, not after they had come
this far.

'And a divorce will give you that?' he'd bitten out
through clenched teeth.

'A separation will.'

There had been a tense silence for a moment, and then
Zeke had said flatly, his dark face an unreadable mask, 'I
don't want my wife living in a hovel, Marianne. I don't
know what sort of gesture you thought you were making,
but you've made it, okay? I can afford for you to live well
whatever happens.'

His hands had been tight on the steering wheel, the
knuckles taut and white, and it had only been that betrayal
of his inward turmoil that had stayed the hot, angry words
hovering on her tongue.

She didn't want his money. Neither had she been trying
to make a dramatic gesture! Why wouldn't he *listen* to
her? Even now he couldn't hear what she was saying. He
was so cold, so unapproachable—his mind was a locked
door and he jealously guarded the key, even from her.

He had only ever given her little portions of himself,

she'd realised suddenly. Just so much and no more. He had compartmentalised his life and she had been allotted her box, along with everything else, but that was all.

That wasn't a marriage; it wasn't even a relationship. She had opened the car door with an abruptness that had surprised them both, her voice weary and strained as she had said quietly, 'Goodbye, Zeke.'

And his voice had been equally quiet and bleak when he'd answered in turn, 'Goodbye, Marianne.'

She had expected the car to roar away the moment she turned away from it, but it hadn't been until she had switched on the light in the bedsit and walked across to the window and begun to close the curtains that it had moved slowly away down the dark, deserted street. And she had gone to bed…alone.

'Oh, Zeke, Zeke.' She spoke his name on a little hiccup of a sob, glancing desperately round the room, which had now become quite cosy from the warmth of the gas fire. 'Please love me like I love you. That's all I ask.'

It was maudlin self-pity of the worst kind, and after a few indulgent moments she flung the duvet aside and jumped up from the sofa.

She wasn't going down that avenue—not now and not in the future, she told herself firmly. She had a job to go to and she needed to be bright and cheerful when serving the customers, not pink-eyed and miserable, however she was feeling inside.

And come the weekend she would make some enquires regarding further education; she wasn't just going to talk about it—she was going to *do* it!

She had never regretted the decision to support her father through the bleak, dark time after her mother's sudden death, but she'd always known she was merely delaying going away to college or university, nor forgetting it altogether. But then Zeke had swept into her life, with all the charisma and drawing power of a powerful being from another world, and things had changed. She had let them change.

She gathered up her toilet bag and towel in preparation for her sojourn in the bathroom down the landing, and then pulled the belt of her robe tighter as her thoughts travelled on.

She had always enjoyed practical chemistry at school, she was more like her father academically than her mother, and her A level results in biology, chemistry and maths had been excellent. Becoming a doctor like her father had been an idea at first, but then, through work experience and contacts of her father, she had been drawn to a career in medical laboratory work. And she could make it happen; it was up to her. There were thousands, *millions* of women who had absorbing, interesting careers and were wives and mothers, too...

Her heart started thudding as her stomach swirled violently. But Zeke couldn't—or wouldn't—see that. And she was losing him. Perhaps she had already lost him. And a world without Zeke would be so empty and pointless that the greatest career in the universe wouldn't compensate—

'*Stop it.*' She spoke out loud, through clenched teeth. She couldn't doubt herself now. She had rushed into her marriage like a giddy schoolgirl and the result had been a disaster. She loved Zeke, she would always love him, but she couldn't go back to how things had been and he didn't see any need for them to be different. He had been so cold and hard in the car last night, so distant and intractable.

The weeks they had been apart hadn't touched him, not deep down. He still didn't see the need for them to talk, to communicate, to *listen* to each other. She had been shrivelling up and dying inside for months and he was oblivious to her despair.

She took a deep, shuddering breath, her hand reaching for the door, and then jumped violently when the buzzer connected to the door in the street sounded in her right ear.

'Marianne?'

It sounded like Zeke's voice, but it couldn't be, she told herself silently as she spoke into the intercom. 'Yes, who is it?'

'How many men could it be at this time of the morning?' came the dry response.

'Zeke? What on earth are you doing here?'

'Freezing my butt off.'

'Oh, I'm sorry. Come up.' She pressed the switch to release the street door and then gazed wildly about, as though her clothes and make-up were going to jump on her all by themselves so she could present a cool, contained façade. There was no time to do anything but hastily fumble in her toilet bag and run a brush through her tangled hair before his knock sounded on the door.

Right, you can handle this. From his attitude the night before he had probably come to dot the i's and cross the t's on their separation, she thought frantically. He was a control freak in every area of his life; that had become more and more apparent through the two years she had been married to him. Always cool and immaculate, with an undeniable air of authority and command that was awesome. It had only been when they were in bed, and he was loving her with every fibre of his mind and body, that she had felt she had all of him. But perhaps even that had been an illusion she had created because she didn't want to face up to the sham of their marriage?

When his knock sounded again she pulled herself together and wiped all trace of her thoughts from her face before she opened the door. And then she stared at him, her mouth falling open in a slight gape before she said bewilderedly, 'Zeke, what on earth…? You're soaked, absolutely soaked. Has the car broken down somewhere?'

'No, the car hasn't broken down,' he said wearily, raking back his hair as the snow covering his head began to melt in rivulets down his grey face. 'I've been walking.'

'Walking?' She could see he was shivering as he stood dripping on the draughty landing, and now she pulled him into the room, shutting the door before saying briskly, 'Get your coat off and I'll switch the kettle on. You need something warm inside you.'

'Marianne?' As she went to move away he caught hold of her hand and his flesh was ice-cold. 'I love you. If nothing else, I want you to understand that. But there's another part of me…' He let go of her, turning away with a savagery that spoke of suppressed emotion.

'Zeke, what is it?' The look on his face frightened her. 'Are you ill?'

'Probably.' He drew a long, shaking breath. 'In here.' He tapped his forehead before turning to face her again, contemplating her wretchedly from beneath his hooded lids, his eyes so smoky dark as to be black. 'When I left you last night I drove back to the apartment and parked the car and then began walking. I needed to think about what you'd said.'

Marianne ignored the fierce stab of hope the last words had given her, and said instead, her voice concerned, 'You haven't been walking all night in this weather? Oh, Zeke, that's crazy. You'll catch your death of cold.'

'That'd be a clean end to this mess, if nothing else,' he said bitterly through the uncontrollable chattering of his teeth.

'Don't be silly.' She regarded him now in the manner of a schoolmarm admonishing a naughty child, although there was nothing childish about the six foot two, big, dark figure in front of her. He looked broodingly sombre and impossibly handsome, but exhausted. And cold, very cold. The last thought caused her to say firmly, 'Get your coat off, Zeke, and hand it here. There's an airer in the bathroom; I'll hang it in there.'

However, once divested of his coat, it was clear he was soaked right through, the designer suit as wringing wet as his overcoat.

'You're chilled to the bone, aren't you?' She couldn't believe that the logical, cold, imperturbable man she had lived with for the last two years could have been so irrational as to walk the streets all night in the worst snowstorm the south had seen for a decade. 'You need a hot bath if you aren't going to catch pneumonia.'

'I'm all right.' It was abrupt. He hated her fussing.

'You're not all right.' It was equally abrupt. She left him standing in front of the fire and walked across to the ancient wardrobe, pulling out her jeans and a jumper. After flinging her dressing gown on the sofa she quickly pulled on the jeans and jumper over her nightie, slipping her feet back into her shoes before turning to face him again, her face flushed.

He was watching her, and as their eyes met and held Marianne felt her heart begin to thud as his dangerous attraction reached out into the space between them. 'I'm going to run you a hot bath,' she said, her voice as firm as she could make it through her wobbly insides, 'and I want you to take everything off and put my robe on.'

'*What?*'

She frowned. 'Don't argue, Zeke.' She turned away from him before he could answer, and reached for the unopened jar of mustard she had bought the day before. 'And this is going in, too.'

'Marianne—'

'I'll be back in a minute, when the bath's ready.' She was out of the door and halfway along the landing before he had time to argue.

She made the bath as hot as human flesh could stand, and once it was full and steaming went back and knocked on the flat door.

When Zeke opened it she willed herself not to laugh, but her voice had a faint gurgle to it when she said, 'The bath's ready and I'd soak for at least half an hour if I was you.'

He surveyed her from under black beetling brows, his limbs sticking out from the heavy towelling outlandishly, and the material straining across his chest and broad shoulders as it stretched at the seams. She had never, in all her life, thought to see the autocratic, imperious Zeke Buchanan in such an incongruous situation, but her amusement was tempered by his grey colour and the way the skin was pulled tight across the chiselled cheekbones.

'You'll need a towel.' As she squeezed past him in the doorway all amusement fled as the powerful hardness of his male body beneath the soft towelling made itself known, and the scent of him—a mixture of many things, but undeniably his—teased her nostrils briefly.

'Thanks.' He took the towel from her as she handed it across with downcast eyes and he was already walking towards the bathroom when she raised her gaze. His big-boned frame, the massive width of his shoulders and the hard line of his back caught at her senses and desire flared, hot and strong, taking her completely unawares.

She bit hard on her lip as she closed the door, her eyes cloudy with unease. As soon as Zeke was anywhere near, all rationale had a habit of flying out of the window, she admitted unhappily. It was that which had kept her beguiled for two years and she had to be on her guard against his magnetic pull now.

Zeke was a devastating strategist and a ruthless opponent, she had seen him persuade people black was white without batting an eyelid, and when those attributes were added to the rest of his fascinating persona… Yes, she had to be very, very careful.

Marianne hadn't expected Zeke to take any notice of her instructions, but it was exactly half an hour to the minute when his knock sounded at the door.

She had boiled some water in the meantime, stripping off her clothes and having a hasty wash in the sink before getting dressed properly and doing her hair and make-up. She could have a good soak tonight, she'd told herself feverishly. For now it was of supreme importance to be in control of the situation, and for that she needed every weapon at her disposal. She had to present a cool, calm front—she wasn't, she very *definitely* wasn't, going to fall into his arms.

That resolve was severely tested when she opened the door to him. In spite of the chill on the landing he hadn't put the robe on again, merely draping the towel around his lean hips with a sight too casual a regard for safety. He was lithe and tanned and thickly muscled, and the tight black curls on his chest and the power in his hard, male thighs made her breathing quick and shallow as she said squeakily, 'Come in, come in,' before moving flusteredly back towards the kitchen area.

'I'm making a hot drink,' she said jerkily over her shoulder, without turning to look his way again. 'It's a pity I haven't got any brandy or whisky to add to it to combat the cold.'

'I'm not cold now.'

Neither was she! For an awful minute Marianne thought she had spoken out loud, but the response had only been in her mind.

'That's good,' she managed brightly, hoping Zeke couldn't see the way her hands were shaking. 'But I'm afraid your clothes aren't even remotely dry yet. Don't...don't you want to put my robe on again?' she added, trying to keep the desperate plea from sounding in her voice.

'No, thanks,' he returned drily.

She turned then—she had to; she couldn't very well continue to fiddle with the teapot and tray for ever, and the hot tide of sensation which had just begun to diminish slightly washed over her again as she met the smoky grey gaze.

The jet-black hair, the hard male jaw, the piercing intentness of his heavily lashed eyes—he was gorgeous! Just too darn gorgeous to be true, she told herself with silent desperation.

'You...you shouldn't risk getting cold again.' His clothes were gently steaming on the back of the sofa, which she'd pulled close to the warmth of the fire, and now Marianne indicated her neatly folded duvet as she said, 'If you don't want the dressing gown, wrap that round you.'

'Marianne, there's things I have to say,' he said huskily.

Fine, but at the moment all she could concentrate on was the way the hair on his chest narrowed to a thin line bisecting his flat, taut belly, and it wasn't doing her equilibrium any good.

She nodded in what she hoped was a brisk fashion, wondering how she could feel so incredibly shy with her own husband, and turned back to the tray of tea. 'Okay, but breakfast first,' she said weakly, adding an extra spoonful of sugar to her mug for much-needed strength. 'Bacon sandwiches all right?'

'Bacon sandwiches sound wonderful.'

His deep, throaty voice made her shiver—he'd always had the sort of voice that would have been pure dynamite on the silver screen—but at least by the time she had set several rashers of bacon sizzling in the pan on the stove and poured the tea, he had draped the duvet round his shoulders.

It helped, a bit, as she passed him his mug of tea and took a nervous sip of her own, but the atmosphere was still so tense and taut that she found it difficult to persuade her throat to swallow.

She risked a glance from under her eyelashes after a few moments of silence, and saw he was looking towards the window, where the snow was still thickly falling, his profile grim. And then he turned his head suddenly, meeting her eyes, and said in a low voice, 'You were right about the separation, Marianne, we both need to think about the future. But I don't want you living here. I want you to have an allowance, okay? Get something decent.'

She wanted to say something, anything, but the shock of his words had robbed her of all coherent thought. *He didn't want her any more.* Here she'd been thinking she would have to repel his advances or something similar, and all the time he had been going to say he wanted the separation. She didn't know whether she wanted to laugh or cry, but as she couldn't very well do either she called on every scrap of strength she had left and said quietly, 'I like it here, and I don't want your money, Zeke.'

'It's not *my* money,' he bit out harshly, and then, as her face whitened still more, he said more gently, 'It's not my money, Marianne. You are my wife; you have certain entitlements.'

Entitlements? She couldn't trust herself to speak. She didn't care about entitlements; she only cared about him, she cried silently. Couldn't he see that? Didn't he understand? She couldn't believe they had come to this.

'I...I'd better see to the bacon.'

As she turned blindly away she thought she heard him murmur something along the lines of, 'Damn the bacon,' but in the next moment the twang of the sofa told her he had sat down, and she decided she must have imagined it.

'You have been very unhappy in this marriage, haven't you?' It was more a statement than a question, and the way he said it made her blood run cold, but before she could respond he continued flatly, 'And now the very thing I feared the most has come to pass; I've *made* it come to pass.'

She breathed deeply and then turned to face him. She didn't understand this conversation, she didn't understand *him*, and whatever else she wasn't going to play games. Things were so bad they couldn't get any worse, so she might as well be honest. 'Zeke, you might know what you are talking about but I haven't a clue,' she said tightly. 'You've just told me you're happy to have a separation—'

'Happy?' he bit savagely.

'Well, aren't you?' she shot back angrily, suddenly furious at how easily he could manipulate her emotions. She had given him everything when they had married—her heart, soul, mind and body—and it made his power over her frightening.

'Marianne—' He stopped abruptly and then rose, flinging the duvet away irritably before walking to stand at the window, the towel low on his hips and his back to her.

The quiver of sexual excitement she had felt in spite of

everything that was happening made her voice brittle as she glared across the room and said, 'Zeke, *talk* to me, for goodness' sake! Shout, scream, do what you want, but I'm sick of the long cold silences that happen every time we discuss us. All the months we've been married and I've tried to talk to you about the house and children and a job and whatever; you do this to shut me up. Well, I won't shut up, do you hear? You can't intimidate me any more because I won't let you!'

'Intimidate you?' He turned to face her then, and his face was as white as a sheet. 'Is that what you think I'm trying to do?'

'Well, what, then?' she shouted despairingly. 'If not that, then what?'

'I can't...' He raked back his hair and she saw, with absolute amazement, that his hand was shaking. 'I can't explain,' he ground out bitterly, 'and not because I don't want to, but because I don't know *how* to. I've never had to talk to anyone, explain anything. All my life I've had to be self-sufficient and one step ahead of everything else. I don't know *how* to let go.'

'But I'm your wife!'

'I know that. Hell, I know that,' he bit out, so harshly she took an involuntary step backwards and almost tipped the frying pan off the stove.

It startled them both, and with a muttered oath Zeke was at her side. 'That's all I need on my conscience,' he said with bitter irony, 'for you to end up in Casualty with first-degree burns on the coldest day for years.' He swiftly turned off the gas.

Quite how she came to be in his arms Marianne wasn't sure; she only knew she wanted to be there. His body was hard and strong, and as she put her hands on his upper arms, felt the hard, bunched muscles beneath her fingertips, she felt such a fierce surge of desire she couldn't contain it.

She met his hungry mouth with a fervent passion that matched Zeke's, and as his hard male body ground into her she moved against him with equal voracity.

One hard thigh pushed between her legs and she folded herself round the thrusting need, his chest creating a voluptuous, crushing pressure against her aching breasts that was pure, exquisite pain.

He was devouring her with his body, his mouth and tongue creating their own magic until she moaned for more.

The towel had long since slipped to the floor and now, as her clothes followed it, Marianne was too bewildered with pleasure to resist.

There was a tight, hot congestion at the core of her and she knew what it portended, and then, as he moved her to the sofa and began to caress every inch of her with his lips and tongue, she arched against him, relishing the familiar feel of his mouth and body.

He was a master of his craft, and as his mouth worked slowly and provocatively over her taut breasts, her belly and down towards the V between her thighs, she shuddered, every muscle straining in the release of ecstasy only he could bring.

Zeke was hugely aroused, but even as she spread slender, supple limbs and urged him into the silken path of her his control held. He continued to touch and taste her until she was almost fainting with the pleasure of it, the rhythmic undulations that began at the core of her gathering greater and greater impetus.

And then he was inside her, possessing her so completely that nothing else in the world existed but the moment, and like an explosive trigger the contractions deepened and swelled until she was floating in another time, another universe, where all was blinding light and sensation.

Zeke gave a fierce groan of shattering gratification at the moment of their mutual climax and their fulfilment was total, their satiation absolute.

They lay for long, indolent minutes wrapped in each other's arms as their flesh cooled from the feverish intoxication, but as reality rushed in with all its crystal-clear brutality Marianne became tenser.

What had this meant to him? she asked herself silently. She knew what it had meant to her—a complete giving of herself, a union so elemental as to be all-consuming. But Zeke? Zeke was a man; he could separate the sexual act from his emotions much more easily.

'Zeke?' It was a tiny whisper, and then Marianne said the words she would normally never have voiced. 'What are you thinking?'

She felt him tense, she even thought his lips touched the tangled silk of her hair for a moment, and then he said very softly, which somehow made it all the worse, 'That this was totally unfair. I'm sorry, Marianne, I should never have touched you.' And then he lifted himself off her, and she felt a desolation so profound as to be indescribable.

CHAPTER SIX

MARIANNE forced herself to eat a bacon sandwich before she left for the supermarket, although every mouthful felt as if it was sticking in her throat.

Zeke, on the other hand, ate his six rounds of bread with half a pound of bacon and lashings of tomato sauce with every appearance of enjoyment, washing it down with two more mugs of tea.

She glanced at him as she pulled on her coat, wishing with all her heart that it didn't thrill her to see him sitting on her sofa, but it did. Which probably made her the most stupid person in all of England, she reflected silently.

He caught her eye, smiling the smile he used so rarely but which had the power to turn her inside out, before he said softly, 'Sure you don't mind me staying a while longer?'

'Not at all.' She tried to sound brisk and matter-of-fact, but it was not easy in view of the fact he was practically naked. 'Just let yourself out when your clothes are dry and you're ready to go.'

'We never did have that talk.'

Story of their lives together, really. 'No, we never did,' she agreed evenly, her throat tight. If he'd ever really intended it, that was.

And then he made her feel guilty for the unworthiness of her suspicions when he said, quite humbly for Zeke Buchanan, 'Can I stay until lunch-time and we'll talk then? We need to get a few things sorted.'

More than a few. She nodded carefully, searching in her

mind for how best to phrase her next words. 'I think it might be better if you came to the shop and we went for a bar snack, something like that,' she managed steadily. 'In view of the separation we shouldn't really be...'

Her voice trailed away as words failed her.

'Copulating?' he suggested expressionlessly.

Okay, pretty basic, but then what had she expected? Marianne asked herself savagely. 'Making love' would have been slightly out of place, in the circumstances, although that was exactly what she had done. And Zeke had copulated.

'I break for lunch at one,' she said stiffly.

'I'll be there.'

Selfish, unfeeling, arrogant pig of a man! She found she was calling him all the names under the sun as she ran down the stairs after a hasty goodbye, and then she stopped just before the door into the street, leaning against the wall for a moment. But he *had* been sufficiently disturbed by what she had said to him the night before to lose a night's sleep, she reminded herself hopefully. That was good, wasn't it?

Or had his nocturnal musings merely confirmed that they weren't suited and should part? He hadn't said anything to the contrary; in fact, if she thought about what he had *said*, rather than what he had *done*, every indication was that he had decided they should part. And she had fallen into his arms like a ripe peach the minute he had touched her! She groaned quietly, the chill from the wall behind her nothing to the bleak rawness that swept through her as she remembered her total capitulation.

When she opened the door she stepped into seven or eight inches of snow, which immediately swamped the one pair of shoes she had brought with her from the apartment. Great, just great. She stared down at her already soaking feet in exasperation. Thank goodness the supermarket wasn't a few blocks away! Well, it looked as if a new pair of boots was on the agenda for lunch-time, as well as her date with Zeke. Or perhaps Mrs Polinkski would let her nip out mid-morning and do a spot of essential shopping? She didn't fancy presenting herself to Zeke as the little waif and stray, especially not after this morning. He needed to see her as cool, calm and confident, perfectly able to take care of herself and her own destiny—not orphan Annie.

Lunchtime saw Marianne snug and warm in the new winter coat and boots which had effectively cleared out the last of her bank account, but she didn't care. Her life was in ashes round her feet, her husband wanted a separation—she ignored the little voice reminding her she had been the one to set the ball rolling—and she had made a terrible mistake in sleeping with Zeke that morning, but she intended to look like a million dollars for this lunch date.

Never mind that it was basically to confirm the end of her marriage and all the hopes she'd had for the future; she would go out of his life like a glittering star, not a damp squib!

It was in that frame of mind that she sailed out of the shop at one, glancing round for Zeke as she did so.

'Marianne?'

She hadn't seen the BMW, parked, as it was, between a large van and a big four-by-four, but as Zeke wound down the window and called to her she lifted a gloved hand—new beige leather gloves which matched the boots and complemented the chocolate-brown coat perfectly—and walked carefully over to the car. It had stopped snowing but was freezing hard, and the pavement was like glass.

'Hallo, Zeke,' she said shortly, her cool voice belying

the rapid beating of her heart as he left the car and walked round to open her door for her.

He had obviously been home to change; the big lean body was clothed as immaculately as ever, a different overcoat open over a crisp designer suit that dared a flake of snow to spoil its spotless perfection. He looked what he was—a powerful, wealthy, handsome man with an excess of intelligence and a raw magnetism that was lethal. As different from the grey-faced, tormented individual she had opened the door to first thing that morning as chalk from cheese.

Would the real Zeke Buchanan please stand up!

As she slid into the car and he closed the door, before walking round the bonnet to the driver's seat, she found herself watching him.

She had seen two facets of his complex personality this morning—one, a tongue-tied, tortured creature, and the other a devastatingly accomplished and confident lover. Now she was seeing a third—the man he usually presented to the world in general. But it was the first one who interested her. She hadn't seen him before, and something deep inside, born of her love for him, told her she had to see that Zeke Buchanan again if there was any hope for them.

He had been very low this morning, exhausted with all his defences down, and so the mask had slipped for a while. She would have to make it slip again.

And she wouldn't do that by dressing herself up as she had this lunch-time and trying to act a part—the part of cool, self-contained woman of the world. She had to be herself, whatever the cost. In fact, as she looked back over the last twenty-six months and saw how much she had tried to clone herself to fall into line with the Lilianas of his empire, she was surprised and shocked at herself.

Zeke had fallen in love with an ordinary young girl who hadn't known one designer label from another, who had been exuberant and fresh and outspoken.

Admittedly that young girl hadn't realised how complicated and perplexing the object of her devotion was, but she was still the young Marianne inside, only with the benefit of more than two years' wisdom and maturity as Zeke's wife. He was hurting badly, he had shown her that in the brief glimpse of himself that morning, and she had to try and get him to open up to her.

It didn't mean she wouldn't go through with her plans for the future; she needed to do that for her own sake. Zeke was too consuming a husband, too dominant for her not to have her own interests and career. She needed that to balance their roles. Their marriage could only benefit from it.

Of course this was assuming she still had a marriage. Her mouth twisted wryly and Zeke, who had just slid into the car and started the engine, said quietly, 'That's a Mona Lisa smile if ever I saw one. What are you thinking?'

The young Marianne would have told him, and so she did. 'I was wondering if you have written us off,' she said baldly.

The car swerved slightly but the male enigma held. 'I rather thought the boot was on the other foot,' he said coolly. 'And they are very nice boots, by the way. You weren't wearing them this morning, were you?'

Very neatly done, she thought irritably. He had sidestepped the issue with a sugar-coated pill to make her sweet. 'No.' She smiled brightly. 'I bought them to impress you, if you must know. Along with the new coat.'

This time he couldn't hide his surprise, the grey gaze flashing over her face for a moment before he said, 'They have. Impressed me, I mean.'

'Good.' She returned to the attack. 'So, have you decided we're finished, Zeke?'

There was a heavy silence for a moment, and then he said, his voice very tight, 'It's not as easy as that, and you know it, Marianne. The bottom line is that being married to me is destroying you, and I see that now.'

'And this morning, when we made love?' she asked, with an evenness that was pure will-power as her heart thumped so hard against her ribcage she was sure it must be rocking the car. 'Because that's what we did, Zeke. We made love. We didn't copulate like a pair of animals or a one-night stand. We made love to each other.'

'That doesn't alter the way things are,' he said coldly.

But she had caught the hidden note of pain in his voice and it gave her the courage to say, 'No, it doesn't; I know that. But things don't have to be that way, do they? You said, when you first arrived at the bedsit this morning, that you loved me. Do you? Do you love me?'

'Of course I love you.'

'There's no "of course" about it,' she said with a braveness she was far from feeling. 'People fall out of love all the time, we both know that, and sometimes it's said as a prelude to letting someone down gently—'

'Hell, Marianne, what do you want from me?' It was a harsh growl, and then, as he braked violently to avoid running into the car in front of them, he said grimly, 'Can't this wait until we're having lunch?'

'No, because you'll shut down again then and I won't even have a snarl from you,' she shot back angrily.

The traffic was stationary, and as the grey eyes swept across her hot face she saw reluctant amusement in the dark depths. 'Is that what I do? Snarl?' he murmured softly.

And she wasn't going to be charmed away from the

main thrust of what she wanted to say either. It had happened too many times in the past and enough was enough. 'Occasionally,' she said evenly. 'If all else fails.'

'I'm surprised you've stayed with me two years, considering your low opinion of me.' He said it lightly, but there was a definite edge there.

'Perhaps it's because I love you,' she said quietly.

'History is littered with people who loved each other and ended up in a hell of their own making.' He met her eyes and held up a hand as she opened her mouth to protest. 'No, you wanted me to talk so I'll try and tell you how I feel, Marianne.'

The lights changed, and as the BMW purred forward he said tensely, the words seemingly wrenched out of him, 'I'm not making excuses, so get that straight from the start, but I owe it to you to tell you how it is; I see that now. It was self-indulgent to marry you. Quite how self-indulgent I didn't realise at the time.'

She sat quite still, her hands clasped together and her eyes staring ahead as she willed herself to listen quietly and show no emotion.

'I'd had other women before you, Marianne, but you know that,' he said grimly. 'They were on the whole confident, perhaps even aggressive, career women: women who knew exactly what they wanted out of life and what they were aiming for, who wanted their personal lives to be controlled and uncluttered. They didn't expect or want the emotional involvement that comes with commitment, but none of them were promiscuous, not even Liliana.'

She inwardly flinched at the name but remained absolutely still outwardly, her face expressionless.

'All they required, as did I, was the assurance that for as long as the affair continued it would be monogamous, with both parties being totally honest.'

'It sounds very cold-blooded,' she said quietly, keeping all trace of censure out of her voice.

'It was.' He nodded sharply. 'I liked it that way. You see, Marianne, the one thing I brought out of my childhood and youth was autonomy. For the first five years after my mother had placed me into care she visited now and again, and at that stage she refused to consider letting me go for adoption. She lived a pretty wild lifestyle by all accounts, and in a strange sort of way I think I was her security blanket.' His mouth twisted cynically.

'Then she met a guy, a rich guy, who didn't want to have someone else's kid in the background, and when he proposed marriage I never saw her again. She signed the papers for adoption then, but I was a disturbed little boy, difficult. I—' He paused, and then bit out tightly, as though he resented having to say the words, 'I missed her.'

Her heart was turning over in pain for him but she was wise enough not to show it. In all the months they had been together his past life had been a closed book to her, apart from the bare essential facts he had told her in the first weeks they'd met. Any approach by herself to discuss his childhood had always met with a firm rebuff and change of subject. 'How old were you when the first adoption attempt failed?' she asked softly.

'Six and a half.'

There wasn't a trace of emotion in his voice, but she now knew that meant nothing. Inside there was still a small hurt boy, and she'd been a fool, such a fool, not to see it. Perhaps if she'd been older, more experienced, when they had met she would have understood better, even persuaded him to show the festering wound the clean, healing light of day? But she hadn't understood. And he hadn't said a word.

'That must have been hard for you,' she said steadily.

'It wasn't too easy on the prospective parents either,' he said with a touch of bitter amusement. 'They had chosen a cute little boy with black curls and a serious face—their description, by the way, not mine—who virtually wrecked their house and turned their neat, orderly way of life upside down. We all made mistakes—I was crying out for help—' she thought it indicative of how damaged he was that he couldn't, even now, say love '—and they reacted in all the wrong ways.'

He glanced at her then, one swift glance, as he said, 'Not that it was their fault. They were just nice middle-class people who didn't have a clue what had hit them. They should have had a sweet little Shirley Temple type girl, not a ferocious little boy with a chip on his shoulder as big as him.'

'And the second time?' she asked carefully.

'That was a year later. I was placed in another foster home after the first adoption attempt failed, and I think I was happier there than I'd ever been or ever was again. They were good folk, kind, and they understood kids. They'd got two boys of their own with learning difficulties but they still took on a couple of foster children and gave them as much time and attention as their own kids. Anyway, I was taken away from them and placed with a couple of virtual strangers who I'd visited a few times on ''little tea-parties'', and I went ape.'

Marianne nodded. She could imagine, and she was filled with burning anger that someone in charge hadn't understood how things really were.

'I think I thought if I played up enough they'd send me back to Marlene and Jim, but of course it didn't work out like that. I was sent to a children's home and told Marlene and Jim had another child living with them and didn't have room for me. I don't think the matron who told me meant to be unkind,' he said flatly, his face hard, 'but it did something to me. Something died, Marianne. Call it the ability to reach out, to be normal. I don't know. But from that point on I stopped needing anyone. I became ungovernable and totally opportunistic; if it wasn't for the fact that I found I enjoyed school and proving I was better than everyone else I'd have probably ended up in Borstal.'

She had been so wrapped up in what he was saying that she hadn't noticed where they were going, but now, as the car pulled up in a small side street, she saw they were close to Rochelle's. 'I don't want to eat at Rochelle's,' she said hastily, without considering her words.

'What?' As he cut the engine he turned to her, the grey eyes narrowed and very dark. 'Why not?'

Because in Rochelle's everyone knows who you are and how much you are worth, she thought with absolute clarity. They'll fawn over us and you'll be Zeke Buchanan, multimillionaire and tycoon. I won't get another word out of you that means anything. She shrugged carefully. 'Myriad reasons,' she said lightly. 'There's a couple of pubs and various eating places all round here; let's leave the car and walk.'

The narrowed gaze moved to the window, where the odd desultory snowflake was beginning to whirl in the wind.

'Not far,' she said quickly. 'Just a little way.'

They found a small bistro on the first corner, and once they had ordered the food and a bottle of wine Marianne leant across the table and said softly, 'Were you telling me in the car that you don't need me, Zeke? Is that what you were saying?' He would never know how much it hurt.

He stared at her, his black hair ruffled from the biting wind outside the warm confines of the restaurant and his grey eyes reflecting the light just above their heads, which turned them almost silver. He had never looked more handsome, or more unapproachable.

She waited, not daring to breathe, for his answer, wondering how everything could appear so normal and mundane when she was crying, screaming inside. She had opened a can of worms that day she had run from the apartment and she didn't know if she was strong enough to bear what he might say. She loved him, she would die loving him, and yet he was a stranger to her. She had lived with him, eaten with him, laughed with him and slept with him, they had shared physical intimacies she had never imagined in her wildest dreams, and yet all the time there had been a huge great chunk of him he had kept all to himself.

Suddenly she was angry, too. He *should* have told her some of this before; it had been her right as his wife to at least know what she was battling against. He had cheated her.

And then, almost as though he had read her mind, he said the exact same thing himself. But suddenly Zeke— her Zeke—was back, and the relief was overwhelming for a moment. 'I'm saying I cheated you, Marianne,' he said heavily, 'but as for needing you…' He looked at her with agonised eyes. 'You'll never know. Not in a million years.'

He shook his head, and then as her hand reached out and gripped one of his he looked down at it for a moment, before raising his head and saying wearily, 'I'll destroy you if you stay with me and I've no right to inflict any of this on you. Don't you understand? I am what I am; I can't change. I knew what I was doing, deep down, when I kept you from finding a job. I wanted to keep you locked away. But then you know that, don't you?'

'Why? Why, Zeke?' she pressed urgently.

'Because I needed to know you were mine, totally, that

you weren't seeing or talking to other men,' he said with shocking matter-of-factness. And then his gaze gripped hers as he said grimly, 'And how does that add up with the rest of what I've been saying, eh? If I could have locked you away, I would have. That's how I felt.'

And until he had met her he had never been plagued by that emotion before, she thought intuitively. He had liked his other women to be independent and self-sufficient, living their own lives and making no claims on him, and then with her a whole new set of feelings had come into play, and it had made him feel weak, confused, vulnerable.

Because of his upbringing he hadn't gone through the normal family ups and downs to knock off the edges and round him off as a person. All the punches life had thrown at him had been knock-out blows aimed straight for the jugular—annihilation and being crushed, or retaliation and militant aggression; that was how he had seen it. Get the other fellow before he gets you. Life on his own terms and damn the rest. And then she had happened.

'Don't you trust me, Zeke?' she asked shakily.

He made a sound deep in his throat and removed his hand from under hers, leaning back in his chair and surveying her broodingly. And then he smiled bitterly. 'My honest little wife,' he said mordantly. 'Nothing swept under the carpet.' He straightened slightly, and then, as the waiter brought their bottle of wine, took it from him with a nod of thanks as he said, 'I'll see to it.'

She waited until he had poured two glasses of the deep red wine, and then she said again, 'Do you, Zeke? Do you trust me?'

'No.'

She had been expecting it, but it still hit her like a blow in the solar plexus. 'Thanks.' She couldn't quite keep the bitterness from showing through.

He looked at her as he caught the note, a long look, and then he took a hard pull of air as he said, 'I don't trust that one day you won't see me as I see myself.'

'And how's that?'

'Unlovable.'

Oh, Zeke. Oh, my darling... She didn't say a word, and she tried, really hard, to keep her face from revealing what she felt, but she obviously failed because he said, his voice harsh, 'And don't feel sorry for me, Marianne, because that will be the last straw. I've made a life for myself and a damn good one; the Buchanan name is both feared and respected.'

His remark about his name triggered a thought, and she forced herself to sit back in her chair and take a sip of wine before she said calmly, 'Is Buchanan your mother's name or your father's?'

'My mother's, before she married.' He took a long swallow of wine himself before he added, with no expression at all, 'I told you; she led a pretty wild lifestyle. I gather my father could have been any one of a number of bozos who got lucky. Certainly no one was willing to claim paternity, and who can blame them?'

You, for a start. 'Has your mother contacted you since you were older?' she asked quietly.

'When I became wealthy, you mean?' His lips tightened and then he breathed out slowly from his nose. 'I'm sure she would have done; she was a mercenary little—' He stropped abruptly, finishing the glass of wine in one gulp. 'She died,' he said blankly. 'Fell off a friend's yacht when she was drunk at a party and drowned.'

Her eyes widened slightly with shock. He had never spoken about his mother except once, when he had told her, on their second or third date, that his mother had given him away as a baby. But she was dead; his mother was dead. That meant there was no chance of any reconciliation or possibility of a reunion.

It was a silly question in the circumstances, but she'd said it before she'd thought. 'Are you sure?'

His features were as flint-hard as his eyes when he said coolly, 'Quite sure, Marianne. I spoke to her husband some years ago and he filled me in on all the gory details of her life. He didn't spare my feelings,' he added drily. 'I was left with the impression they'd deserved each other.'

'I'm so sorry, Zeke.'

He shrugged. 'Don't be.' And then, as he glanced over her shoulder, 'Ah, here comes the food.'

He regretted telling her everything; she could tell. She stared at him as the waiter placed their meals in front of them. But she wasn't going to stop battering at that wall he had built between them.

'What if we'd had a baby, Zeke? What then?' she asked quietly once they were alone again.

'A baby?' There was just the tiniest inflexion in his studiously flat voice that made her look at him more intently. He *wanted* a child, she realised suddenly. He had always wanted a child, perhaps even more than she did. And she could understand why now. A tiny little being that was no threat, that wouldn't turn away from him or fall out of love with him, that would be linked to him through the blood as well as the heart.

And he would be a devoted father. He would lavish love and tenderness on the flesh of his flesh, knowing he could do so without appearing weak or vulnerable. He didn't have to trust a baby not to leave him, and whatever happened he would still be its father.

'It didn't happen, did it?' he said with smooth control. 'Which is probably just as well in the circumstances.'

'I agree.'

As his eyes shot to meet hers she saw it was not what he had expected her to say.

'We weren't ready to have a child, Zeke,' she said softly but clearly. 'We still had too much growing up to do ourselves.'

'Is that a dig at me?' he bit tightly, his skin stretching over the rugged lines of his face.

'No, I said both of us and I meant both of us,' she said firmly. 'You called me honest a while back, so you can't have it all ways. I believe that every child should have the right to be conceived through love and born into a loving and trusting relationship. There might be some people who would disagree with that, but I can't see it any other way. Trust, love, tenderness, commitment—they should see all that mirrored in their home, Zeke. I've grown up a great deal in the last two years and I've had to sort out what *I* want and what *I* believe, not what my parents or society or anyone else tells me.'

'And all this growing up told you to leave me.'

'It told me we couldn't go on as we were,' she said sharply. His voice had been dry and cynical. 'I'm a person in my own right, Zeke, with dreams and aspirations, but that doesn't lessen my love for you an iota. I don't have to be just a wife, or a wife and mother and nothing else, don't you see? You can only benefit if I'm happy and fulfilled.'

'And being my wife wasn't fulfilment enough,' he said tightly.

'No, it wasn't.' Her hands were trembling with the enormity of their differences, and she linked her fingers together to stop their shaking. 'Like being my husband isn't enough for you. You have your work, which consumes you at times. Admit it.'

'That's different,' he said harshly.

'Why? Because you're a man?' she challenged swiftly. 'What rubbish, Zeke. You know as well as I do that a woman can be just as dedicated as a man to her work.'

'We'd agreed you were going to have children and I'd be the breadwinner,' he shot back roughly, changing his tack in view of her scathing voice.

'And the children didn't happen.' She eyed him firmly. 'And you know as well as I do that you don't have to do another day's work in your life and you'll still be a multimillionaire for the rest of your days.'

'This is a ridiculous conversation,' he said crisply, dark colour flaring across his countenance.

'Why? Because you are hearing a few home truths?'

'That's enough, Marianne.'

'And now you're shutting down again because you aren't winning.' She was looking at Zeke and he was looking back, his eyes narrowed and hot and his mouth a thin line in the tautness of his jaw.

She had gone as far as she could for one day. Marianne followed her instinct and, despite the churning of her stomach and the trembling in her limbs, smiled brightly. 'Think about what I've said, Zeke,' she advised calmly, willing her voice not to shake. 'You are telling yourself you can't change because you are too scared to try, and out of that has come a whole cart-load of hang-ups. Whatever you might think, I love you, and I shall continue to love you as long as I live. I could be the next Prime Minister and I'd still love you—a top model, whatever.

'You exasperate me at times, annoy me, drive me mad, if you want to know. And you're right—you *have* cheated me. You've cheated us both, actually. But I still love you, more than ever. Because love, real love, doesn't choose where it wants to go; it just happens. There's no rhyme or reason to it very often, and certainly it defies logic. But it happens and that's that. *Fait accompli.*'

She had expected some dry, cynical barb at the end of her little oration, one of the razor-sharp cuts that he did so well, and her stomach muscles had clenched in readiness. But he just sat there, his expression frozen and revealing nothing of what was going on in his mind.

And then, as one of the young waiters bustled over, enquiring if their food was to their satisfaction, Zeke made some polite comment on their as yet untouched meals and they both began eating.

But Marianne had seen his hand shake slightly as he transferred a forkful of food to his mouth, and that, more than anything else that had occurred, gave her the slightest ray of hope.

CHAPTER SEVEN

MARIANNE had expected—perhaps foolishly, she acknowledged to herself as she sat at the bedsit window watching a frosty Christmas Eve dawn—that Zeke would be in touch after their frank and somewhat caustic meeting that snowy December lunch-time.

Admittedly she had received an outrageously generous cheque through the post from his solicitors two days later, along with an official note stating the same amount would be repeated on the fifth of every month, and asking could Mrs Buchanan please inform Jarvis & Smith of her new address in due course? She had returned the cheque the same day, with a short note stating that she did not intend to change her address, neither did she want the money.

After that, sixteen days ago, she had heard nothing from the solicitors and nothing from Zeke.

Her father had been to see her twice and taken her out to dinner, and on the first occasion—once the initial awkwardness was over—they had talked as they hadn't done for a long time. By the time he had left she had known he understood how things were, and on his second visit they had simply enjoyed each other's company, which had been great.

Pat had come to stay for a couple of days the week before—complete with army sleeping bag which she'd insisted on spreading out on the floor at the side of the sofa bed, refusing Marianne's offer to use the sleeping bag herself—and the two of them had had a girly weekend which had done Marianne the power of good. You simply couldn't wallow in self-pity or any other negative feelings with Pat around.

And Mrs Polinkski—bless her—seemed to have made it her mission in life to make sure Marianne was well-fed and befriended, inviting her to their spacious flat above the supermarket for a home-cooked meal several times a week, and always insisting the son of the family—Wilmer—saw her home to the door of the bedsit, despite Marianne's protests.

Marianne frowned as her thoughts unfocused her gaze on the winter sky of silver and pale peach. She might have something of a problem brewing with Wilmer, actually, she told herself darkly. The Polinkskis were fully aware of her situation, but in spite of that Wilmer had asked her out for a drink twice in the last few days, and despite her refusals seemed more keen, if anything. He had taken to looking at her with great sad puppy-dog eyes and making unnecessary visits into the front of the shop every two minutes. It was beginning to drive her mad.

He was a nice enough boy—he was probably her age, but seemed heaps younger to Marianne—and quite good-looking, with his shock of dark blond hair and brown eyes, but, apart from the fact that she was a married woman, she could never have liked him in a romantic sense in a hundred years.

All in all, life had been full and busy—she had barely had time to look through the university and college prospectuses she had sent away for—so the gnawing feeling of aloneness which hadn't left her since she had first walked out of the apartment was silly, ridiculous, *crazy*. But it was still there, she admitted with a deep sigh as her eyes focused on the river of mother-of-pearl and varying shades of luminescent peach again. And it was worse, if anything, when she was with people. All she wanted, all she seemed able to think about whatever she was doing or saying outwardly, was one particular person.

'Oh, Zeke.' She spoke his name out loud, her breath misting the cold glass before she rubbed at it with the sleeve of her dressing gown. He had admitted to a profound emotion for her that was all at odds with the rigid control he liked to keep on his feelings, and in the voicing of it had made it impossible for them ever to go back to the old way of things. Not that she would have contemplated that herself, of course.

Nevertheless, the portent of all they had said that lunchtime had the power to blow their marriage to smithereens or ultimately make it stronger than it had ever been, but it all depended on Zeke. And she didn't, she really didn't, she reiterated miserably, know which way he would jump.

Christmas Eve. She looked up above the frosted rooftops and then shut her eyes against the brilliance of the early-morning sky. Last year Zeke had worked until nearly five, despite giving his employees the afternoon off, and she had spent most of the day wrapping presents for him, which she'd placed under the little tree she had bought, and getting a sumptuous festive meal for the two of them and a couple of friends he'd invited round. They had eaten in the intimidating dining room and she had hated every minute of it, mainly because just before the friends had arrived she'd discovered that her late monthly cycle had been another false alarm and her hopes had been crushed again.

Since her mother's death her father had taken to spending Christmas with his small army of brothers and sisters, most of whom lived in Scotland, and for the first two Christmases—until she'd met Zeke—she had joined him. However, Zeke had been reluctant to take any more than two or three days away from his empire—or that was the excuse he had given for not leaving London and their apartment—and so their Christmases had been short affairs, filled with his friends and acquaintances.

He would receive masses of invitations for Christmas Eve parties and Christmas lunch; he always did, she thought soberly. Along with drinks here and there, and Boxing Day soirées and so on. And if word had got out that they were living apart and he was 'available', there would be more than one eagle-eyed female willing to provide a shoulder to cry on. In fact they'd be queueing for miles.

Her mouth tightened at the thought and she brushed back a wisp of fine, silky silver-blonde hair from her cheek. His silence over the last two weeks might be indicative of the fact that he had decided to avail himself of female comfort, and she could use up all her fingers without even trying in counting certain women in their social circle who would be aching to provide it.

Marianne sighed heavily and rose to her feet, her face as pale as alabaster from her musings. She missed him so badly. Missed waking up beside him and seeing him, relaxed in sleep, more like the serious-faced little boy with black curly hair he had spoken of at their last meeting. Sleep ironed out the cynical lines of his hard face, mellowing his features and bringing emphasis to his thick dark lashes and firm, beautifully moulded mouth. And his body... She shut her eyes tight for a moment and then opened them, walking across the room with what amounted to a grim expression on her face now. She wasn't going to think about him right now; *she wasn't*. She could do all her moping later.

She had a long, leisurely bath and washed her hair before getting dressed for work, some perverse determination making her pull on the bright red jumper the faithful old charity shop had provided a few days before, after which she tied her hair high on the top of her head in a jaunty ponytail, securing it with a red velvet ribbon.

She had decided to spend Christmas at the bedsit, despite numerous invitations from her father and his relatives, Pat and her family and Mrs Polinkski, so she wasn't going to belly-ache about it now. Her husband had obviously decided to call it quits, she didn't have two pennies to rub together and Christmas dinner was going to be a turkey sandwich, but what the hell! She had two arms, two legs and she was in her right mind—there were others who were much less fortunate.

The little pep talk helped—a bit—but her eyes were still gritty with unshed tears as she ran down the stairs half an hour later and opened the door into the street.

'Zeke!' He was standing there, right in front of her, and for a moment she felt herself go weak at the knees at the sight of him. She stared at him as if her eyes were deceiving her, and she noticed the lines etched round his eyes and mouth appeared deeper and he looked thinner overall.

'Hallo, Marianne.' It was cool and contained, but she had seen the hot glitter in the grey eyes in the moment she had opened the door and taken him by surprise. 'I wanted to talk to you.'

'I'm just on my way to work,' she said breathlessly, and then, in case he thought that was a refusal, she added quickly, 'But they won't mind if I'm a few minutes late.'

His eyes had been moving over her flushed face and wavy, silky hair, and now he touched the red ribbon with one finger as he said thickly, 'I like that. You look like a Christmas sprite this morning, bright and glowing.'

'Do I?' Zeke was the last person in the world given to fanciful compliments and it threw her even more.

'Yes, you do,' he said softly. 'And very beautiful.'

'Thank you.' She gestured backwards with a trembling hand. 'Do you want to come up for a minute?'

'That's not necessary, I don't want to make you late for work.'

She stared at him uncertainly. This big, powerful and very sexy man was her husband, and yet she didn't have a clue what was going on in his mind.

'The reason I came…' He paused, and she realised with a little shock of surprise that he was nervous. It hit her like a bombshell. 'It's just that your father said you weren't spending Christmas with him when I spoke to him last night.'

'Did you expect me to?' she asked evenly.

'I suppose so. Yes, I did,' he added suddenly. 'Or with Pat or other friends. But Josh said you intend to have Christmas on your own here.'

'He shouldn't have phoned you,' she said tightly. Zeke's pity she could do without!

'He didn't. I phoned him,' Zeke said shortly. 'I—I wanted to make sure you were all right.' And then, before she could say anything, he raked back his hair irritably in a gesture she recognised only too well, and said angrily, as though she had forced it out of him, 'In actual fact I wanted to see if there was a possibility we might meet some time over Christmas, but I didn't know if you would be around or if you'd feel like it.'

'Couldn't you have asked *me* that?' she asked steadily through the mad beating of her heart.

'I wasn't sure if you would want to speak to me,' he said with brutal honesty, 'not with the way things are. The separation means you are free and I didn't want to complicate things or embarrass you.'

She didn't know whether she wanted to kiss him or hit him! 'You haven't embarrassed me, Zeke,' she said carefully, trying to ignore the shaft of pain that had pierced her heart at the 'free' statement. 'What had you in mind?'

He shrugged warily, his eyes roaming over her face again, and she suddenly found herself longing to reach out and touch him, to feel his arms about her. She curled her fingers into fists and buried them deep in the pockets of her coat to restrain herself.

'I haven't made any plans either,' he said, even more carefully than her, 'so perhaps dinner tonight?'

'Everywhere will be packed Christmas Eve.' She took a deep breath, praying for courage, as she continued, 'Why don't you come here and I'll cook us something?' Mrs Polinkski would sub her for the food out of her next wage packet.

And then he took care of that detail when he smiled at her with his eyes and said, 'As long as I provide the food and the wine?'

'It's a deal.' How could everything that had been so wrong be so right in a few moments of time? she asked herself silently. Suddenly the day was transformed, beautiful, and all because she was going to see him tonight. It was hard to contain the wild beating of her heart; even though she knew how dangerous it was to hope she couldn't help herself. And he had agreed to come *here*, to her little bedsit. A few weeks ago she couldn't have imagined him doing that, not when he had been so furious at her leaving the apartment.

And then something of the glow left the morning as he said, quietly and very matter-of-factly, 'And I know this is no strings attached, so don't worry.'

No strings attached? She wouldn't object to all the strings in the world! Or perhaps she would? Oh, she didn't know—she didn't know anything when Zeke was around.

He had the power to turn her upside down and inside out with just a glance of those devastating grey eyes.

'I'll walk you to the supermarket,' he offered coolly, and then, as she fell into step beside him, he said politely, 'How are you enjoying working there?'

If she had answered truthfully she would have told him it was boring and allowed her far too much time on quiet days to daydream about him, but instead she said brightly, 'Oh, the Polinkskis—who own it—are very nice. I think Mrs Polinkski looks on me as one of the family now; she's even hinting at my continuing there when her daughter comes back from Poland in a couple of weeks' time.'

He nodded, his profile aloof and distant, and she found herself wondering if he was regretting agreeing that she cook for them that night. And perhaps it was too twee and cosy at that? she thought worriedly. And how on earth was she going to cook anything worth eating in the archaic oven that had a mind of its own? And the tiny table would just about carry two place settings and nothing else; it certainly wasn't going to be a dignified affair, with candles and bowls of this and that.

Of course she could fetch the bamboo screen back in from where she'd placed it in the bathroom—she'd dispensed with its services as soon as she'd moved in, finding it just got in the way—and hide behind that while she dished the food up, but it wasn't going to be easy. Oh, why hadn't she thought of all the consequences before she'd thrown caution to the wind?

'What time do you finish work?'

They had reached the shop and he turned her briefly to face him, his hand dropping from her elbow almost immediately.

'Four. I'm working through my lunch hour because Mrs

Polinkski says the world goes crazy from about eleven to three and then we're shutting shop at four.'

They were talking as courteously as two strangers. He *was* regretting this evening, she thought miserably. She stared up into his dark face, searching for the right words to tell him he didn't have to come, and that she perfectly understood how he felt about things—the comments relating to her freedom and no strings being attached had been crystal-clear—when he bent quickly and kissed her.

It was a hard kiss, and passionate, and certainly couldn't have been mistaken for a friendly goodbye. One hand was clasping the back of her head and the other arm was wrapped round her back, and she could smell the intoxicating fragrance of him as he held her close to his hard male frame. The scent released a thousand erotic memories, and as the desire to moan against his lips rose overwhelmingly she jerked away, horrified at his power over her.

'They…the Polinkskis might be watching,' she stammered jerkily. 'They know I'm separated and they might…might think—'

'And they might think you're a scarlet woman with a secret lover?' he teased drily, but with a gentleness that made her sigh with relief that she hadn't offended him.

'You never know,' she said with unintentional primness.

'No, you never do,' he responded with a quiet smile that made her want to leap on him. 'I'll be waiting at four, okay?'

'Okay.'

And then he was gone, striding back down the street to where the BMW sat waiting, and she turned into the shop, her heart perfectly in tune with the joyous carols that met her ears from the supermarket's speakers.

*　*　*

Zeke was back before four—just gone one, to be precise—
and as she glanced up from serving another of the steady
stream of customers that had filled the shop all day,
Marianne felt her heart stop and then race on at express
speed.

He looked cool and indifferent to the Christmas throng,
the original ice-man, and she was so sure he was going to
cancel their date that her mouth fell open in a little gape
when he bent down and said, very quietly, in her ear, 'Can
I borrow your front door keys?'

'What?' She was aware of Mrs Polinkski and Kadia,
who were manning the other two tills the small shop
boasted, watching them interestedly, and she knew she was
blushing a bright scarlet.

'Your keys,' Zeke repeated patiently. 'I've bought a few
things and I'd like to leave them in the bedsit if that's all
right?'

'Oh, yes—yes, of course. I'll just...' She gazed round
somewhat desperately. 'My bag's in the back.'

'I can wait a while.'

She found it excruciatingly hard to concentrate on what
she was doing, with every tiny sensor in her body aware
of Zeke as he leant lazily against the far wall, his dark
gaze trained on her hot face, but eventually she finished
serving her customer, asked the next in the long queue to
wait for a moment, and flew out to the back of the shop.

He levered himself upright as she reappeared, taking the
keys with an enigmatic smile as his eyes lingered on her
mouth long enough for her to feel hot all over.

'I'll see you later,' she whispered feverishly, aware of
their audience as Mrs Polinkski's and Kadia's eyes burnt
a hole in her back.

He nodded. 'Till four.'

It was typical of Zeke that he didn't waste any words.

When he spoke it was brief, concise and succinct, she thought ruefully as she watched the big dark figure walk out of the shop without a glance at anyone, regal and autocratic to the last. And then she caught at the wayward feeling of tenderness the thought evoked, forcing it under lock and key before it could run riot.

She loved him, but nothing had changed, not really, she told herself firmly. They might be sharing a Christmas meal tonight but they were separated still, and it didn't look as though Zeke was any nearer to dealing with his personal demons.

But he *had* come to see her, the reckless, more abandoned Marianne breathed radiantly. He could have spent Christmas with any one of a number of besotted females, but he had sought her out. That meant something, didn't it?

Pity? A feeling of responsibility? Guilt? the sensible little voice in her head said nastily. It could mean any one of those or all of them.

Or it could mean he hadn't been able to stay away. But the radiance was dimming as the sensible part of her came to the fore.

She took a deep, steadying breath and turned back to the next customer, who had been watching events with some interest.

'Your young man, is he, love?' the little old lady with bright round button eyes and rosy-red apple cheeks asked in a stage whisper. 'Bit of all right, ain't he? Reminds me of my 'arry, he does.'

Marianne glanced at the pitifully meagre items in the basket, which included a roast turkey dinner for one, and as though the little woman guessed what she was thinking, she added quietly, 'Lost 'im in the War, love. We'd only bin married six months. Over fifty years ago now, but I never married again—although I had offers. Oh, yes, I did an' all.' She nodded her head like a bright-eyed robin. 'But no one measured up to my 'arry, if you know what I mean.'

'Yes, I know exactly what you mean,' Marianne said softly.

'You make the most of each day, love. That way you won't 'ave nothin' to reproach yourself for. Me an' my 'arry, we packed a lifetime of lovin' into a few short months, an' I've no regrets. There's not many as can say that, eh?' the tiny old lady said with a cheeky grin.

Marianne smiled back, although she felt more like howling, but one thing had clarified in her head. She was right to let Zeke come tonight, however things turned out. Like the little old lady's beloved Harry, no one could measure up to Zeke. He was a one-off, and if they didn't get back together again she would have to face living life alone for the rest of her days.

She'd do it—she gave a grim mental nod to the silent declaration—but she didn't want to. Oh, *how* she didn't want to.

'Mrs Perry?' Mrs Polinkski had come bustling across to Marianne's till as her other daughter came to take over the lunch-time stint. 'You won the raffle, dear. Did you know?'

'Did I?' The rosy red cheeks expanded further as the little woman beamed at Mrs Polinkski. 'Well, I never. First time I've won a raffle in me life.'

Mrs Polinkski glanced at the giant hamper on display at the front of the supermarket and then back to the diminutive elfin figure in front of her, and said kindly, 'I'll call Wilmer and he can take you home in the van, Mrs Perry. There's a nice fresh turkey to go with it, you know.'

Marianne glanced at Mrs Polinkski—the turkey hadn't

been part of the prize but was typical of the generosity of the other woman; Mrs Perry was a favorite among the Polinkskis—and smiled. People could be so *nice*.

'A turkey?' Mrs Perry was clearly enchanted. 'By, this'll be a Christmas to remember all right. I'll call in an' ask me friend, Ada, to come for Christmas dinner, an' we can make a party of it.'

'You do that,' Mrs Polinkski said cheerily, 'and a very merry Christmas and happy New Year, Mrs Perry.'

The warm glow Mrs Perry's good fortune gave Marianne continued for the rest of the afternoon, and when—at just gone three—Mrs Polinkski gave her a very generous Christmas box in the form of a cheque, and told her she could leave early, she didn't need telling twice.

She could put the bedsit to rights before Zeke came, she told herself as she hurried along the frosty pavement, although no amount of tidying or titivating could make it other than what it was. But it didn't matter. Nothing mattered. Because she was going to see him tonight!

She knew she ought to curb the fierce surge of pleasure and excitement that had been mounting all afternoon but she couldn't, she just couldn't, and anyway—it was Christmas. Everyone was allowed to hope and dream at Christmas, after all, and even though she knew she might be building her hopes on shifting sand, it couldn't quell her happiness.

This would be the first Christmas Eve they had spent with just the two of them, she realised as she neared the house. And it also might be their last. She didn't like the cold little voice of reason that seemed determined to pop up at the oddest moments that day, and she was frowning as she dived into her handbag for her keys.

And then she remembered. Zeke had them.

Oh, great. She glanced at the shutter window of the

charity shop and sighed. Wonderful start. She hadn't given the keys a thought, not even when she had asked Mrs Polinkski to keep an eye open for Zeke and to send him along.

There was just the merest chance someone from the charity shop might be sorting stock in the spare room on the landing, although she doubted it. Nevertheless, she rang the bell on the off chance, and then gasped out loud a moment later when Zeke's voice said, 'Yes, who is it?'

'Me.' And then she added hastily, 'Marianne. It's Marianne, Zeke. But what are you doing here at this time?'

'I could say the same to you,' the rich dark voice said back. 'It isn't four yet, is it? Not by my watch anyway.'

'I left early.'

This was ridiculous—standing in the freezing cold on her own doorstep talking to the occupant of *her* bedsit!

The same thought must have occurred to Zeke, because in the next moment the door whirred and clicked open and then she was running up the stairs, quite unaware of the brightness of her eyes.

He was standing in the bedsit doorway as she reached the landing and she noticed he was dressed casually in an open-necked charcoal-grey shirt and trousers. She would have liked to pretend she was oblivious to the dark, virile masculinity, but the wild racing of her blood said otherwise. Nevertheless, she managed a fairly composed, 'Hallo, Zeke,' as he smiled at her.

The surprise of finding him there coupled with the excitement she was trying to hide made her work on automatic as he waved her past him into the room beyond, but she had taken no more than two or three steps when she came to an abrupt halt, her eyes widening and a sense of unreality taking hold.

The dingy little room was transformed. A small Christmas tree complete with tinsel and baubles and twinkling lights stood on the table, the battered tabletop hidden by the gaily wrapped parcels covering it. And that wasn't the least of it.

In one corner of the room a TV was relaying an afternoon carol concert at some cathedral or other, the strains of 'While Shepherds Watched their Flocks by Night' filling the air waves. Marianne stared at it incredulously, too amazed to speak or move.

In the limited kitchen area boxes of groceries stood waiting to be unpacked, along with several bottles of wine, a small turkey, two enormous one-inch thick steaks, and cartons of mushrooms, tomatoes and other fresh produce.

A large bowl of fruit and another of mixed nuts stood either side of the little gas fire, which was casting a warm glow into the room, and with the fading light outside the small bedsit had gained a cosy cheerfulness it could never aspire to in the harsh, searching light of day.

'Zeke?' She turned to face him, utterly bemused, and as her eyes met his she could find nothing to say, not even thank you. She just couldn't believe that he had done all this for her; taken time away from his precious work schedule and the thousand and one things which claimed his attention to be here.

'The TV's your Christmas present, before you object,' he said softly. 'That's not breaking any conditions of the separation, is it?'

His eyes were almost black in the dim light, with tiny dancing flames from the reflection of the fire, and his hard mouth was twisting in a smile that was very self-deprecating. He looked big and dark and all male, and the force of her desire frightened Marianne to death.

She dropped her lids and fought to gain control of her

feelings. 'I don't suppose so,' she said carefully, her voice trembling a little. 'But I haven't got anything to give you.'

He didn't reply, and then, as she lifted her gaze to his dark face and saw the look in his eyes, she knew the heat which had begun in the core of her was staining her cheeks deep pink.

It was Zeke who broke the moment, which had become electric, as he turned towards the food, saying, 'I couldn't get all I would have liked to without a fridge, but I dare say we can survive on that lot for a couple of days.'

'A couple of days?' she queried warily.

'You wouldn't deny a starving man Christmas lunch?'

'You don't look starving.' He looked, well, he looked sensational, she thought weakly.

'No?' The hunger she had seen in his eyes a few moments before was even stronger as he turned to face her fully again. 'Looks can be deceptive,' he said with wry dark humour, a strange little smile playing about his hard mouth.

Their eyes met and held, and Marianne felt her heart begin to beat faster and faster. 'Zeke—'

'No, don't say anything,' he said softly, moving swiftly to her side as she stood looking at him uncertainly. His hands cupped her face gently before his fingers stroked some errant strands of silky curls back from her temples. 'Don't say a word, Marianne. Can't we take the next two days as something apart from real life? We won't talk about the past or the future, just live hour by hour in the present and pretend we're the only two people in the world.'

She stared at him, her hands resting against his broad chest, and she could feel the rapid beat of his heart beneath her fingers. The twinkling lights from the little Christmas tree and the warm rosy glow from the fire brought the magic of Christmas into the room, and she knew she wasn't going to resist him. Mrs Perry had said she'd made the most of each day with her Harry and that she had no regrets, that she'd packed a lifetime of loving into just a few months.

She had two days, and she was going to make the most of them. It might be crazy—it was almost certainly crazy, considering he hadn't made any promises and nothing between them was resolved—but she was going to do it anyway.

She drew a long, shaky breath, and then lifted her hand to his mouth, tracing the firm lines of his lips with one finger. 'Kiss me, Zeke.' It was an answer in itself.

'The heart has its reasons which reason knows nothing of.' She had read that somewhere recently, and as Zeke's mouth took hers she embraced the thought. She loved him; nothing else mattered.

He was kissing her deeply and passionately, and as she wound her slim arms round his neck and kissed him back, fiercely, he growled low in his throat, causing her to arch further into the taut hardness of him.

They undressed each other with feverish, frantic haste, and then they were naked in the dim light of the shadowed room, her slender body pale against the darkness of his tanned male flesh. He was unashamedly aroused, and as his hands roamed her body she gloried in the power she had over this big, ruthless, powerful man. He wanted her and she wanted him, wanted to feel the silky hardness of him inside her and know that she was joined to him in an act as old as time itself.

He was breathing hard, his broad, hair-roughened chest rising and falling as he fought for control, and then he moved her to arm's length, in order to drink in the sight of her. She stood in front of him proudly, her head uplifted to his gaze as his hungry eyes moved down the pure line of her throat, the full, rich ripeness of her breasts with their jutting peaks, the flatness of her smooth stomach and long shapely lines of her legs.

'Beautiful. So, so beautiful,' he murmured thickly, his voice shaking. 'I want you so much...'

She stepped forward and rubbed herself against him with a brazenness she had never displayed before, and, inflamed by her boldness, he picked her up in his arms, carrying her over to the sofa and laying her gently on the coverlet. She lay stretched out before him, loose-limbed and pliant, and he knelt down on the rug and took the hardened tip of one breast into his mouth as his hands caressed her flesh.

The pleasure was so piercing as to be unbearable, and as she writhed and moaned his hands and mouth continued to caress and kiss every inch of her until she was trembling uncontrollably, her head moving frantically from side to side in a vain effort to combat the exquisite sensations he was drawing forth.

When he joined her on the sofa she was more than ready for him, utterly surrendered to the raging passion that had taken him over. He drove himself deeper and deeper into the moist, delicate sheath, and the contractions that had had her panting beneath his lips and hands exploded into a glorious, tumultuous release for them both, the world shattering into a million pieces.

They lay quietly afterwards, Marianne circled close in his arms as the flickering firelight played over their en-twined bodies, and as a deep lassitude swept over her Marianne let herself slip into it. She was aware of the steady beat of his heart, the intoxicating, familiar feel of hair-roughened flesh against her smoothness and the sweet murmur of carols from the TV in the background, but it was all like a warm blanket covering her senses.

How long she slept she didn't know, but when at last she roused herself it was to the knowledge that the curtains were drawn against the dark sky outside and she was wrapped round with her duvet.

'Zeke?'

'I'm here.' He answered immediately, and when in the next moment he stepped into her vision she saw—with a touch of wryness—that he had come expecting to stay. Although the short towelling robe could hardly be called clothing, it was more than she was wearing beneath the duvet, and she suddenly felt unaccountably shy.

'Don't move; I'll be right back.' He grinned at her as he ducked away, reappearing almost immediately with an opened bottle of wine and two glasses, which he placed on the floor next to the sofa. 'Move over.'

He discarded the robe with magnificent unconcern for his nakedness and joined her beneath the duvet before reaching down and pouring two glasses of the deeply coloured and fruity red wine, which smelt of damsons and spices. 'I vote we spend Christmas just like this,' he said huskily, the lightly rough friction of male skin against female arousing them both. 'With brief visits across there for food and drink, of course, which we can then eat here too. What say you?'

With his arm about her shoulders and her head resting against his chest she could only nod her agreement; words were quite beyond her at that point. If this wasn't heaven on earth she didn't know what was.

Later, after they had loved some more, Marianne cooked the steaks while Zeke prepared and tossed the salad, as naked as the day he was born, and then they snuggled under the duvet again and ate the meal watching the classic film *Scrooge* on TV, with another bottle of wine.

It was an enchanted Christmas.

Marianne was conscious, as each hour slipped by, that she was in a stolen bubble of time. The joy of waking on Christmas morning and seeing his dark head next to hers on the lumpy old sofa bed was the best gift she could have had, but he had bought her numerous presents, which they opened together over toast and tea which Zeke made.

They loved and ate and drank, and loved some more, almost rendering the turkey into a burnt crisp as they lost themselves in each other's bodies. Zeke's loving was urgent and hungry, as though he couldn't get enough of her, but she didn't let herself think that it might be because he was sensing time was short. As always when they touched each other the need was overpowering, taking control, doing away with the need to talk or communicate beyond the moment.

Even the weather conspired to make the time more chimerical and dreamlike, the snowstorms which had been forecast arriving with a vengeance early Christmas morning and turning the outside world into a blurred white cloud beyond the window.

It couldn't last, of course.

Marianne had known that all along, but the end came with an abruptness that catapulted them both back into the real world with shocking suddenness.

It was late Boxing Day afternoon, and Marianne had been lying drowsily in Zeke's arms watching a silly cartoon on TV, when he nuzzled her head with his chin. 'I've another present for you,' he said softly.

'Another present?' She watched him in surprise as he rose and padded across to his coat, appreciating the way his long, lean body moved with powerful male grace. 'Zeke, you shouldn't have. You've already given me so much.'

'This is different.'

His eyes were narrowed and very smoky as he handed her the envelope—she remembered that afterwards. Almost as though he was already concealing his thoughts from her. As he might have been.

'I don't understand. What's this?' She stared at the envelope as he resumed his place beside her, his face hidden from her gaze as he pulled her comfortably against his chest, her head resting in the hollow of his throat.

'Open it and see,' he said lazily. 'It won't bite.'

'The Bedlows property?' She stared at the wad of documents in her hands. 'You've bought the Bedlows property?'

'You wanted it, didn't you?' he said softly. 'Now I've got it for you.'

'When? How?' She twisted in his arms, her eyes bright and her face radiant. 'Oh, Zeke, Zeke!'

'We should have moved out of the apartment as soon as we were married; I realise that now,' he said quietly as he looked into her excited face. 'It was unfair of me to expect you to live there.'

'It doesn't matter!' She flung her arms around his neck, her voice animated and high. 'Oh, Zeke, Zeke, I can't believe this. You've bought it! It's ours.'

'You're pleased?' He was watching her very closely.

'Of course I am.' She beamed up at him, careless of the way the duvet had slipped down to her waist, exposing the firm high peaks of her breasts. 'When did you buy it?'

'A few days after you had been to see it.'

That should have warned her. If she had been in her right mind that should have warned her, she told herself afterwards, but as it was she didn't understand the portent of the statement. Not when she was held in Zeke's arms and he had just given her a sign that he was going to meet her halfway.

But it wasn't halfway. It wasn't even a tenth of the way.

'I can't believe this.' She felt as giddy as a schoolgirl. 'It's so beautiful and we'll be so happy there; I know it. Of course I shall have to find out which colleges are within commuting distance; I don't want to leave you for days on end, do I?'

And then, even before he said, 'Leave me?' in a flat tone of voice, she knew. Something in his face told her.

'Marianne, this is going to be our home,' he said softly, his eyes holding hers as she shrank back against the sofa. 'It will be a new start, a new beginning.'

'And that doesn't include me furthering my education or getting a job or anything like that?' she said very carefully, her heart thudding and the bile rising in her throat.

'You're my wife,' he said roughly, his voice terse. 'I'm giving you the house of your dreams—'

'I don't want a doll's house, Zeke.' She didn't have to think about the words; they came straight from her heart. 'Neither do I want to go back to the way things were. I'm a person, I'm real, I'm *me*; not a wife doll you can keep in a little compartment in your life. I love this house, of course I do, it's the perfect home, but we are more important. Things have got to be right between us.'

'So it's got to be just as *you* see it, no compromise,' he said accusingly, biting out the words.

This was so unfair. She stared at him, her eyes huge in the shocked whiteness of her face. And then she slid from beneath the covers, pulling on her dressing gown as she rose to her feet and stood looking down at him with tortured eyes. 'I want to *do* something with my life, Zeke,' she said painfully. 'That doesn't mean I don't want to be your wife and have a family, of course I do, but that might not happen for years and years. And what about when the children are at school? Do you expect me to sit at home twiddling my thumbs and just living for the moment when you all come home?'

'You're painting it in the blackest way possible,' he ground out between clenched teeth.

'No, I am not,' she said evenly, her mind racing but crystal-clear. 'You still don't trust me, do you? You still think I might be attracted to someone else if you can't lock me up in an artificial world of your own making. You said, when we talked before, that something died in you when you were a child. I don't believe that. It might have become stifled, buried, but it's there, Zeke, and it's essential for our marriage.'

'You're saying that unless I give you exactly what you want you will end our marriage.' His vice was icy cold. She could hardly credit that it was the same man who had been loving her for the last forty-eight hours.

'Don't twist my words like that.' She was angry and bitterly disappointed. 'I'm saying that I have to be able to breathe and be me, just like you do. I *want* to go into medical laboratory work; it fascinates me and I know I'd be good at it. You and any children we might have would come first, of course you would, just as I'd expect that same degree of commitment from you. Your empire—this wonderful ''thing'' that you have created—actually isn't what life is all about, believe it or not! You don't have to prove yourself, Zeke. Not with me.'

She hadn't meant to say that last bit, it had just popped out of its own volition, but now the impact of her words whitened his face and he rose savagely from the sofa, walking across the room and beginning to pull on his clothes as he said, his voice harsh, 'You've never really loved me, have you? It's been a sham, all of it.'

'Don't you *dare* say that!' She had never before been in the grip of a rage that made a red mist rise before her eyes, but she was experiencing the phenomenon now. She must have walked across to him—she couldn't have flown—but she had no memory of it. 'Don't you dare. I love you. I'll never love anyone but you, if you want to know, but that doesn't mean I'll let myself be submerged. I want to be loved for *myself*. I want you to be proud of anything I achieve, not threatened by it. I want you to support me, for any children we might have to be our joint responsibility, not a means of tying me to the house.'

'Oh, so you actually remember the house now?' he snarled sarcastically as he finished dressing and turned fully to face her. 'This wonderful house that you wanted above anything else?'

'It's only bricks and mortar, Zeke.' His cold eyes had brought a devastating emptiness into her heart that was reflected in her bleak face. 'You are more important—our relationship is more important—than any house.'

'How noble,' he said derisively.

'No, it's not noble,' she said very quietly, her face deathly pale. 'Just love. A few weeks ago you said you'd destroy me if I stayed with you and that you couldn't change. What you are offering me is no different to what you were offering then, however you have convinced yourself otherwise. I have missed you every bit as much as you have missed me, but lying to ourselves is not the answer. The house is not the issue, children are not the issue, your work is not the issue—don't you *see*? And if we start again under false pretences and you do destroy me with your jealousy—'

'So it's all me!'

'Yes, it is,' she bit back with equal ferocity. 'And I won't be bought or silenced with the offer of a doll's house or anything else. Your other women were happy to take you on the terms you offered—perhaps a sterile relationship suited them as much as it does you; I don't know— but I want more. I want *you*. I don't expect you to be perfect—I know I'm not!—but I want you. All of you. Not the little bit you've offered me in the past.'

'How can you say that after what we've shared the last couple of days?' he said angrily.

'That should be my line, Zeke.' The stark bitterness brought his gaze shooting to the chalk-whiteness of her face and her wounded eyes. 'You came here knowing exactly how you were going to play it for maximum effect, didn't you?' The breath caught painfully in her tight throat but she forced herself to go on. 'I don't know if you thought you were buying me or fooling me or blackmailing me or what, but I can't live like you want to live. Not any more. And if you have any real feeling for me at all you won't ask me.'

'I love you, Marianne.' His voice reflected her own agony and she almost softened. Almost.

'If you love me, Zeke, really love me like I love you, you'll trust me enough to give me my freedom,' she said huskily. 'Trust that I would come back to you of my own free will, without having to be kept in a beautiful gilded cage. Trust me enough to talk to me about your innermost fears and know that I wouldn't put you down or think any the less of you for being human. You should be able to give me everything, as I've given you everything.'

'You don't understand.'

'No, I probably don't, not completely. Because you won't let me,' she said sadly. 'But I'd like to.'

There followed a silence so profound she didn't dare break it. This was it. This was make or break time, she told herself silently as her senses clamoured and her mouth went dry. Let him just reach out, just the slightest...

'I'd better go.'

She heard the words, the tight, clipped tone registering on her bruised mind, but she didn't really take them in until after he had reached for his coat and overnight bag. And then she stood taut and still, enduring the light kiss on her forehead and his muttered, 'I'll be in touch,' with just a nod and a raising of her chin.

At the last moment he turned in the doorway and looked at her, and for a moment, a second, she thought he was going to change his mind. He cleared his throat, and the dark-haired, serious-faced little boy was very evident when he said, 'I shouldn't have come, should I?'

She stared at him, willing herself not to break down. 'I don't know, Zeke,' she said, with a flatness that spoke of bitter anguish. 'Only you can answer that.'

He flinched visibly. 'I'm a mess, Marianne, aren't I?' It was not really a question, and didn't require an answer, but the unmasked desperation in his grey eyes hit her like a blow.

Nevertheless she stayed exactly where she was, although every fibre of her being wanted to fly across the room and take him in her arms. He stared at her, his face setting as the seconds ticked by, and then he said, his voice so low she could hardly catch it, 'I would still like you to have the house, no strings attached. It...it'll be a good place for you to start again.'

'The house was a package.' Her voice was very flat; it was either that or scream at him. 'It would mean nothing without you. Sell it or live in it. I don't care.'

'Marianne—'

'Just go, Zeke.' Another moment and she would break down completely. 'Please.'

And he did just that.

She waited until she heard the outer door bang shut and then sank down on to the sofa, her face awash with tears and the pain in her heart unbearable. Christmas was over.

CHAPTER EIGHT

MARIANNE saw the New Year in at a party at Pat's parents' house with her father, and during a quiet moment in the somewhat rowdy proceedings she filled Pat in on all that had happened since she had seen her last. She wished she hadn't afterwards.

Zeke had never liked Pat, and Marianne knew her friend fully reciprocated the feeling, but she had expected Pat would try to understand all the complications that went hand in hand with their split. Not so.

'He's a male chauvinist pig and you're well rid of him if you want my opinion,' Pat said firmly. 'A typical "keep 'em barefoot and in the kitchen". He won't be happy until you're under his thumb.'

'It's not like that, Pat. Really.'

'No? Get real, Annie. He manipulated you at Christmas and he'll try and do it again, you mark my words.'

Marianne glanced at her friend's scowling, obstinate face and was wise enough to change the subject. Pat didn't understand. How could she? She herself had been Zeke's wife for over two years and she barely had a handle on the thing.

'So, what are you going to do?' Pat asked a little later in the evening as they sat down with a plateful of food each. 'Divorce him?'

Marianne's stomach turned right over and suddenly she wasn't hungry any more. 'I don't know,' she said carefully, 'but I suppose it will come to that. For the time being Mrs Polinkski has offered me a permanent job until I start college somewhere in the autumn. I'm looking into which one, out of the four I've narrowed it down to, would give me the best offer—or if any will,' she added ruefully.

'With your A level results? They'll snap you up,' Pat said positively. 'They like a few mature students anyway, looks good on their records.'

'Oh, thank you so much! I'll take my walking stick and hairnet with me, shall I?' Marianne said drily, both girls laughing.

'So you're definitely going for it, then?' Pat was suddenly serious.

Marianne answered with equal solemnity, 'You bet your sweet life I am, Pat.'

'And you're not going to take a penny from him? You're mad, Annie. It'd make life so much easier, and he's rich enough not to miss a few hundred thousand. He'll be laughing all the way to the bank.'

'I don't think he'll be laughing, Pat.' And then Marianne raised her hand as Pat went to say something more. 'Let's agree to disagree about Zeke,' she said very quietly. 'I love him, Pat. I shall always love him but I can't live with him, okay? Subject closed.'

Pat glanced at her friend's straight face, sighed and then nodded. 'Fair enough,' she said flatly, 'but not even a teeny-weeny allowance?'

'Pat!'

'My lips are sealed.'

When she returned to London on the third of January Mrs Polinkski had a parcel for her. 'From your husband,' the plump, motherly woman said conspiratorially.

'Zeke came here?' Marianne bit her lip. 'When?'

'The day after you go to see your father,' said Mrs Polinkski, her accent very pronounced in her earnestness.

'I tell him where you were, that you were going to the big party with friends and relations, and he asked me to give you this when you return.'

'Thank you.' Had Zeke spent New Year's Eve at home alone, or had he had company? It was a thought that had tormented her all the time at Pat's parents' party. Or perhaps he'd gone to the theatre followed by a small, select dinner party? That was the way they had spent the previous New Year's Eve.

When she opened the parcel she found it contained a mobile phone and a note written in his crisp black handwriting.

My solicitors tell me you returned the second cheque I sent you three days ago, which is absolute foolishness, Marianne.

The writing became almost savage at this point.

However, I can't force you to accept what is rightfully yours if you don't want to. If you insist on living in that place at least let me sleep easy at night knowing you have some means of communication with the outside world. I'm seeing to the rental so please humour me and use the damn thing. Z

As a love letter it wasn't exactly flowing poetry, but as Marianne gazed down at the package she felt as touched as if it had been. And then she wanted to cry and shout and wail, to stamp her feet and have a major paddy at the absolute waste of it all. Instead she took off her coat and started work.

That evening, once she was comfortable on the sofa with a mug of coffee, she dialled the apartment's number. She

would be formal and businesslike, she told herself as her
heart pounded so hard it echoed in her ears. Just thank him
for his thoughtfulness, assure him she would use the
phone, and leave it at that. No asking him how he was or
any kind of social intercourse.

When there was no answer she felt such a keen disappointment it necessitated a five-minute talking-to about her
stupidity.

She tried again an hour later, and then once more at just
gone ten o'clock, and this time the receiver at the other
end was picked up fairly swiftly.

'Hallo?' It was a woman's voice, soft and gurgling with
an American accent. 'Can I help you?'

Marianne found she was gripping the telephone so
tightly her fingers were hurting, but after a panic-stricken
moment—when she almost pressed the button to finish the
call—she forced herself to say calmly, 'Is it possible to
speak with Mr Buchanan, please?'

'Zeke? Sorry, he's in the shower,' the Marilyn Monroe
lookalike—if voices were anything to go by—fluttered
sweetly. 'Can I give him a message?'

I'm surprised you aren't in there with him! The words
were on the tip of her tongue, and, horrified at herself,
Marianne said quickly, 'Oh, just tell him Marianne says
thanks for the phone,' before immediately ending the call.
She stood for a moment, the phone held to her chest and
her heart thudding sickeningly, and then she turned the
phone right off. If Zeke called back—if—she wouldn't be
able to be civil.

This does not matter; it does not. When she found herself pacing the room she stopped abruptly. She was the
one who had forced the separation when all was said and
done, and Zeke was perfectly entitled to have women

friends back to the apartment—hundreds of them if he so wished! She had no right to complain or object.

She shut her eyes tightly and took a deep breath, forcing her hands, which had been clenched into tight fists at her sides, to relax.

After turning on the TV she ate a whole box of chocolates which Wilmer—with dewy eyes—had presented to her at Christmas, but the feel-good comfort factor didn't work. She just felt slightly queasy now, as well as furiously angry.

And then she gave up all pretence of reasonableness, had a good cry and called Zeke every name under the sun, and a felt a little better. But not so much better that she could sleep that night.

At three in the morning, when she still hadn't had a wink of sleep, she padded across to the kitchen area and made herself a mug of milky cocoa. She took it back to bed with her, along with half a package of chocolate biscuits—which she ate with a *que sera, sera* disregard for her waistline—and a good book, and resolved to put every thought of Zeke Buchanan out of her mind. It didn't work.

Later, after watching the night sky outside the window give way to the first pink tentative fingers of dawn, she went along the landing and ran herself a hot bubbly bath. She lay for a long time in the warm silky water, her thoughts spinning and whirling, before she washed her hair.

Her body lotion brought more thoughts of Zeke—he had always taken great pleasure in smoothing cream on to every inch of her body—that made her angry at her own weakness and she shed a few more hot tears.

'Enough.' She glared at her pink-eyed reflection once she was back in her room. 'You are going to look great today, as though you haven't got a care in the world. Zeke is not the be-all and end-all of your existence! Understand?'

The reflection nodded obediently, and after another long, narrow-eyed, critical stare Marianne set to work. She dried her hair in thick, silky waves about her shoulders, leaving it loose for once, and then gave herself a manicure. She painted her nails—fingers and toes—in bright, challenging red. She didn't particularly like the shade—it had been part of a Christmas present from Pat—but it suited her mood this morning.

Nails finished, she pulled on a thick cream jumper and a fitted bottle-green corduroy skirt which finished a couple of inches above her knees, teaming them with her new boots, and then set to work on her face.

Subtle golden-brown eyeshadow and mascara deepened her cornflower-blue eyes to violet, and in a spirit of recklessness she used the lipstick which matched the nail varnish Pat had given her.

There. She gazed at herself again in a searching appraisal that was very analytical. She looked young and bright and attractive, she decided, as her blue eyes shone back at her. A woman who knew where she was going and what she wanted, and who intended to have fun getting there.

Her lashes dropped, hiding her eyes as she turned away from the mirror, and not for the world would she admit to herself that she was disturbed by what she saw. She had started this ball rolling, and no matter how fast it gathered momentum she had to see it through to the bitter end, she told herself silently. She just wished that a situation she had thought at one time was so straightforward and clear hadn't turned into such a giant tangle, that was all.

Marianne felt a little self-conscious as she walked into the shop that morning, but she threw back her slim shoulders and smiled blithely when Wilmer—who was wheeling a stack of tins through from the warehouse—give a low, approving whistle at the sight of her.

'You look happy this morning,' he said softly as he stopped at her side. 'And very lovely. But then you always look lovely.'

'Thank you.' She gazed back at him and wondered why she couldn't have been attracted to someone like him in the days before she had met Zeke. He was young, good-looking, virile—so why wasn't there the faintest trace of a spark?

'Marianne...' He hesitated, and then said quickly, 'It's my birthday today and I wondered if you'd come out for a drink this evening?'

Oh, no, not again. She had really thought he'd got the message by now. 'This evening? Oh, I'm sorry, I can't—'

'This lunch-time, then?' he put in swiftly. 'Just a drink between friends to celebrate?'

'As friends?' she emphasised gently, feeling she had to make it perfectly clear where they stood.

'As friends.' He smiled a trifle bitterly. 'I know how you feel, Marianne, so don't worry. I won't embarrass us both by pressing my case.'

'Oh, Wilmer, I'm sorry. It's just that...' She didn't know how to put it.

'You still care about him.' He didn't have to mention Zeke by name; they both knew who he was talking about.

She nodded, unaware of how her mouth had drooped and the shadow in her eyes.

Wilmer stared at her for a moment, wondering what sort of cretin would let a woman like Marianne go, and then he sighed resignedly. 'I think he's crazy, Marianne, but then you know that,' he said lightly. 'And for what it's worth there's always a shoulder here to cry on if you need it. A friendly shoulder, nothing more, okay?'

'Thank you.' And she meant it.

'And now we've had this little chat, can I take it you'll be accepting a few more invitations to dinner?' he probed determinedly, but with a grin to soften the words.

She blushed at that. She *had* been chary recently of going for a meal every time Mrs Polinkski had invited her, in an effort to spare Wilmer's feelings.

He turned away without waiting for a reply, calling over his shoulder as he went, 'Lunch-time, then. And you can buy the first round, considering you haven't got me a card.'

Marianne nipped out mid-morning to the little paper shop halfway down the street and bought a cheeky card she knew would amuse him, but as Wilmer and his father had gone to visit a supplier she had to content herself with waiting until lunch-time to give it to him, whereupon he roared with laughter.

They were still smiling at they left the supermarket, Wilmer pulling her hand through his arm as they began to walk down the wet, cold street and Marianne's face uplifted to his as he grinned down at her. And then she froze, quite literally froze, as Zeke's voice came from a taxi purring gently at the kerb. 'Marianne?' It was cold, gritty. 'Could I have a word?'

'Zeke, what on earth are you doing here?' He was only a couple of feet away from her in the taxi with the window wound down, but she would have walked right by if he hadn't spoken.

That thought had obviously occurred to Zeke, too, as his icy voice reflected. 'What do you think?' he bit out harshly with a searing glance at Wilmer. 'I'm here to talk to my wife.'

She felt Wilmer tighten at the side of her, and now her

voice was rushed as she said, 'I'm just going to lunch. It's Wilmer's birthday.' It wasn't the most tactful way to defuse what had become an electric moment but she was utterly out of her depth.

'I see.' Zeke's eyes were almost black with dark emotion and his mouth was a thin white line.

He had clearly put two and two together and come up with a wacking great ten, Marianne thought dazedly, and she was just going to explain who Wilmer was and that they were work colleagues when she caught the words before they left her tongue.

What was she doing? she asked herself incredulously. Zeke had been entertaining little Miss America last night— she didn't have to explain a thing to him! Talk about one rule for him and one rule for her. How dared he object to anything she did when he was seeing other women again?

'What was it you wanted?' she asked tightly, purposely keeping her arm linked through Wilmer's as she met the granite gaze without the flicker of an eyelash.

'It doesn't matter.' Zeke smiled a grim smile that wasn't a smile at all. 'It'll keep until you're less busy.' The tone was insolent and insulting, and as Wilmer tightened still more Marianne pressed his arm in warning, but it was too late.

'There's no need for that,' Wilmer said sharply. 'We're having lunch, that's all.'

'Sure you are.'

It was lethal and meant to provoke, and now Marianne said hastily, 'Please, Wilmer, I'll join you in a minute, okay? Just give me a moment or two with him.'

'*Him?*' Zeke looked ready to explode as she walked over to the taxi, but with the memory of a breathlessly sexy voice in her head Marianne found she didn't care. There were double standards and there were double standards, but this was something else! 'I'm not a "him", I'm your husband,' he said icily.

'Well?' Wilmer had started to walk slowly down the street as she reached the taxi's window, and Marianne's voice was low but cold. 'What do you want?'

'You phoned last night,' Zeke grated tersely.

She certainly had! 'I left a message with your...friend,' Marianne said pointedly. 'There was no need to talk further. I merely wanted to thank you for the mobile phone.'

They stared at each other for a moment and she saw he was furious, his features rigid. She waited for him to speak, and then when the silence stretched and lengthened began to turn away.

'This is an example of the great love you have for me?' he bit out savagely in the next second, inclining his head down the street in the direction of Wilmer's stiff back. 'It didn't take you long to accept a little comfort, did it?'

'It's not like that.' She glanced at him, her blue eyes sparking. 'And who are you to talk anyway?' she added bitterly.

'What does that mean?'

'What do you think it means?' She was trying desperately to maintain her poise and keep her voice low, but she was so angry she wanted to hit him. 'The little cheerleader you invited back to the apartment last night was there just to talk business, I suppose?' She raised her eyebrows sarcastically, her eyes glinting.

'The what?' And then his eyes narrowed and his mouth compressed before he said, his voice curt, 'Suzy is the wife of the guy I was playing squash with when I fell and broke my ankle last night. She joined us at the hospital and they insisted on seeing me home and getting me a meal before they left. She answered the phone whilst Andy was standing by in case I needed any help in the shower.'

She knew her mouth had fallen open in a slight gape as her eyes left his face and took in the plaster cast on his left foot, but she had never felt so awful in all her life.

She had jumped to the worst possible conclusion, she realised painfully, without considering that there might be a different explanation. And she had objected because *he* didn't trust *her*!

'I…I'm sorry.' She raised her eyes back to his tight face as she spoke. 'I thought—'

'It's quite obvious what you thought, Marianne.' It was icy. 'And I think your lunch date is getting impatient.'

'He's not my lunch date, not in the way you mean anyway,' she said feverishly. 'He's Mrs Polinkski's son; I work with him.' She could tell by the look on his face he didn't believe her.

'How cosy,' he snarled savagely.

'We're just friends,' she said desperately. 'That's all.'

'Very good friends, I'd imagine, from the way you were looking at each other,' he said brusquely. 'You know he's crazy about you? But of course you do,' he added with cynical bitterness.

'Zeke, listen.' She didn't know how to reach him.

'Have you slept with him?' he asked in a strange voice.

'Slept with him?' She was aghast. 'Of course I haven't slept with him.' How could he ask that. How could he?

'But he wants you in his bed.' It was a statement, not a question. 'Is he part of the freedom you're asking for, Marianne? A tall, young, blond Adonis willing to fall at your feet in humble adoration?'

The bitterness was so acidic she could taste it, but her angry retort was checked before it left her lips, the recollection of how she had felt last night suddenly very real. Jealousy was like a canker, eating away at everything good and souring even the best of memories with its destructive influence.

She had been jealous of Liliana, and again last night, and she had felt like hell both times. Admittedly she had thought she had good reason, but so did Zeke right now. And she could appreciate his suspicious resentment of Wilmer in the circumstances; that was understandable— normal, even. It was the other side of the coin, his fierce obsession with keeping her utterly to himself, that had been so detrimental to their marriage.

He had called himself unlovable, and she knew the fear he had that she would leave him for new interests or men stemmed from his loveless childhood; she could even understand his forebodings up to a point. But giving in to them—and him—was not the answer, although she was beginning to wonder if there *was* an answer.

'Wilmer does want me, yes.' She bent slightly as she spoke through the taxi window. 'He's made that very plain. But he also knows there is no hope at all because *I* have made *that* plain. To sleep with another man I would have to love him with all my heart, that's the way I'm made, and my heart is irrevocably yours. You don't believe that but it's the truth. I can't prove it to you beyond what I've said and done already, but if it's going to take years and years of us living apart until we're middle-aged or beyond to convince you then you are more of a fool than I thought.

'I'm not going to not have friends because you see them as a threat, neither am I going to vegetate and lead a monotonous life when I can use my brain to good purpose. You have to accept that for us to have any future together.' She stared at him pleadingly.

'And if I can't?' Zeke said grimly. Their eyes met and held for some moments before he repeated bitingly, 'If I can't, what then?'

'Then you've ruined my life as well as yours,' she stated fiercely. 'Think about it, Zeke.'

He had started to say something else when she turned and walked away, but she didn't check her steps, neither did she glance back towards the parked taxi.

Marianne thought about Zeke and worried about him all the time for the next few days. How bad was the fracture to his ankle? Was he able to sleep? Was he eating enough? He would loathe and detest being anything less than one hundred per cent fit, that was for sure, and patience was definitely not one of his virtues.

Eventually she telephoned Sandra Jenkins, Zeke's secretary, at home and poured out her concern.

'He's fine, Mrs Buchanan, don't worry,' Sandra said reassuringly. 'Like a bear with a sore head, but he's been like that ever since you two parted,' she added ruefully.

'You won't mention I phoned?' Marianne entreated.

'Not if you don't want me to.' Sandra sighed, and there was a moment's silence before the secretary said, her tone tentative, 'Mrs Buchanan, it's none of my business, but you do know he thinks the world of you, don't you? I've worked for Mr Buchanan for ten years now, and the girl-friends he had before... Well, let's just say when he met you I saw a side to him I'd never have dreamt existed. He really loves you.'

'Thank you, Sandra.'

Marianne's voice had been husky, and again the secretary hesitated before she said, 'I hope you both work things out, Mrs Buchanan. I'd hate to see two lovely people lose each other.'

Marianne changed the subject then, asking after Sandra's family to combat the pain in her heart, and they chatted for a minute or two before ending the call.

'He really loves you.' Sandra's words rang in her head as she made herself a cup of coffee. If only it was as simple as that. She wasn't sure if Zeke loved her too much or not enough. Whatever, the end result was the same. They were separated, and somehow, since Christmas when he had given her the envelope containing the deed to the Bedlows' property, she was losing the ability to think they would make it.

She had caught herself once or twice lately thinking in terms of a future without him, and it scared her to death that she could accept that. But maybe she would have to. Perhaps she would have to learn to live alone permanently? She shivered, her blood turning to liquid ice. But she couldn't, she *mustn't* give in to the temptation to capitulate to his terms. She would be miserable and ultimately it would be the death knell on their love. She recognised now that for the last few months of their marriage she had been getting more and more resentful and bitter, and she didn't want to go back to being that person again.

'Oh, what a mess.' She spoke out loud, rubbing her hand wearily across her face. She loved him. She loved him with an all-encompassing love that wanted the best for him as well as herself. But what if he really was unable to escape the darkness and come into the light? The thought was so gut-wrenchingly painful she couldn't bear it.

CHAPTER NINE

IT WAS another three weeks before Zeke contacted her, but
Marianne had been determined the first move would come
from him.

She had gone over and over their last words in her mind
until she could have screamed, but one thing was absolute.
He had to decide how he saw the future with regard to
their relationship, and he had to see it clearly.

The Saturday morning in early February was damp and
cold, but Marianne had spent it at the library, researching
current data on haematology and serology. She had found
she needed to do something constructive to avoid dwelling
on Zeke every spare moment, and the fact that she had
taken her A levels over four years ago meant she was
behind the times on scientific developments, which could
change month by month. She found the research absorbing,
and facts and figures were buzzing in her head during the
walk home to the bedsit in the drizzly rain.

Once ensconced in front of the small gas fire she found
her eyelids closing, and she must have slept, because when
the buzzer sounded she awoke with a start, totally disorien-
tated for a moment.

Her wristwatch told her it was three in the afternoon,
but the murky weather had already darkened the sky to
charcoal, and she switched on the light as she clicked the
intercom and said, 'Yes? Who is it?' in a voice still groggy
with sleep.

'Zeke.'

Just one word but it was enough to send her heart racing

and the blood singing through her veins until she thought her ears would pop. 'Just a moment.'

She leant against the wall and took several deep breaths in an effort to gain control. *He was here.* Now. She flicked the switch to open the door downstairs and then breathed deeply a few more times, telling herself she was being ridiculous.

She only had time to run her fingers through her hair and smoothed down the bubblegum-pink cardigan before his knock sounded at the door to the flat. She opened it at once, her calm face and quiet demeanour betraying none of the surging panic and excitement she was feeling inside.

'Hallo, Marianne.'

Hallo, Marianne. Just like that. Smooth and cool. The words and the tone in which they had been spoken—along with his imperturbable face—registered like a punch in the solar plexus, but she managed to reply in like vein, her voice equable as she said, 'Hallo, Zeke. How's the ankle?'

'Fine.' He didn't smile and neither did she.

It wasn't fine, it couldn't be, but she didn't argue the point, merely standing aside and gesturing for him to enter.

He was limping slightly as he walked into the room but she knew better than to fuss, merely asking, 'When did you have the plaster off?' as she closed the door and turned to face him.

'Yesterday afternoon.' Zeke could never be bothered with trivialities and his tone made this quite clear.

She flushed slightly as their gazes held; he looked good enough to eat and the magnetic quality to his dark good looks had never been stronger. His black hair was damp from the misty rain outside and longer than he normally wore it, indicating he hadn't bothered to get it cut recently. A few errant strands had dared to curl down on to his forehead and it softened the harsh lines of his face considerably. She felt her heart turn over.

He looked big and dark and controlled, his grey eyes narrowed and glittering as they fixed on her and his mouth taut in the chiselled bone structure of his face.

'How are you?' His voice was soft and it sent a shiver snaking down her spine.

'Okay.' She managed a smile but it was difficult.

'Ask me how I am,' he said grimly.

'How are you?'

'As miserable as hell.'

Her heart jumped up into her throat before subsiding back into her chest, where it began to thump against her breastbone so hard it hurt. She wanted to say something but her mind had frozen; all she was conscious of was the look on his face and the nearness of him.

'I love you, Marianne. I can't live without you and I can't take another day of this damn separation,' he said huskily, his voice deep and low. 'When I saw you with that guy…I wanted to do murder. If I'd been able I'd have been out of that taxi and had him by the throat when you first walked through the door of the supermarket.'

She stared at him, stunned by the naked emotion in his voice and the way he was allowing her to see his vulnerability. 'It…it was a good job about your ankle, then,' she managed at last, trying to alleviate the intensity of the moment. She had wanted her voice to sound light and teasing but it was merely shaky.

He nodded slowly. 'If I was noble and self-sacrificing I'd let you go; you know that, don't you?' he said bitterly. 'You deserve someone like that boy, young and fresh and with no hang-ups. Someone you can have fun with, act crazy with, someone with no responsibilities or ties of any kind. You said once there was more to life than Buchanan Industries and of course you are absolutely right. But I have commitments to the people who work for me,

Marianne, whose livelihoods are tied up with the success
or otherwise of the business.'

'I know that,' she said quickly, her voice trembling.
'And I wouldn't want you to give up any part of your
business. You've worked so hard to get where you are.
But...'

'Yes?' His eyes hadn't left hers for a moment.

'You could let go a little more, delegate at times,' she
said carefully. 'You have some good executives working
for you—they have to be good to survive at Buchanan
Industries! You needn't be there so early in the morning
and work so late.'

'Maybe.' He still had made no move towards her.

'And...and me?' She didn't want to ask, she just wanted
to fly into his arms and believe all was well, but she
couldn't. She needed and loved him more than life itself,
but she was still frightened of the future. 'You would be
happy for me to go to college and train for a career, Zeke?'

A muscle moved in his hard jaw but the devastating grey
eyes didn't blink. 'You want the truth?' he asked grittily.

She nodded, terrified of what she was going to hear.

'I don't want you to see or speak to anyone but me,' he
ground out painfully. 'That's the truth. I'm working on it,
Marianne—hell, you couldn't call me anything I haven't
called myself—but I'm not there yet and I can't pretend.
But...' He paused, and for the first time since he had
walked into the bedsit she saw his face relax a little. 'I
know that would be no good for you and you'd be unhappy, desperate. Reason says I want you to be everything
you want to be, and my heart says the same thing; it's just
in here—' he tapped his forehead with a hand she saw was
shaking '—when I start thinking, imagining what it would
be like if you left me—'

'I won't.' She moved to him then, but still he didn't
take her into his arms, his body rigid. 'I couldn't.'

'You can't say that,' he said bleakly.

'I just did.' She stared up into the dark handsome face and found herself wondering for a moment how this man, this powerful, fabulously rich, wildly handsome man, who only had to snap his fingers to have women fighting over him, could be so destructively insecure. And what he saw in her that made him love her so passionately. 'Could you leave me?' she asked gently. 'Could you walk away from me for someone else?'

'That's different.'

'Why?' she pressed softly. 'Why is it different?'

'It just is,' he ground out with painful flatness.

'Zeke, if you hadn't come here today, if we had carried on living apart for months, years, decades, I still wouldn't have wanted anyone else but you,' she said softly. 'Don't you *see*?'

'I'm trying.' It was wrenched out of him, and now he pulled her violently into him, crushing her mouth beneath his as his hands moved hungrily over her body. 'Believe me, I'm trying.'

Marianne responded blindly, the lonely weeks since Christmas making her desire white-hot as she tangled her fingers in his dark hair, matching the urgency of his need movement for movement, kiss for kiss, as they stripped the clothes from each other in feverish haste.

'I've missed you. Hell, how I've missed you.' He held her trembling body away from him for a moment, his arms outstretched and his hands spanning her slender waist as he drank in the sight of her womanly curves and hollows. 'You're so beautiful, so incredibly beautiful, my love,' he said huskily.

'So are you,' she whispered shakily, gasping at the air as the powerful masculine body in front of her filled her vision and took away her breath.

And then she was in his arms again, their hands and lips

moving over each other and creating burning rivulets of desire. She could feel the thrust of his body against her softness and as his knee parted her legs she pressed into him, accepting his manhood into the moist warmth between her thighs as he lifted her off her feet and she wound her legs round his hips.

Sheer molten ecstasy was sending contraction after contraction radiating from the very centre of her being, and as she felt him shudder and then emit a hoarse groan of pleasure, the world shattered into a million brilliant pieces beneath her closed eyelids and she found herself in another dimension, another universe of exquisite fiery sensation.

She wasn't aware she was crying as she felt him draw shuddering breath after shuddering breath, deep into his lungs, their bodies locked together and her head buried in his shoulder. And then, as she raised her head and looked into his face, she felt the salty hot trail down her face.

'I love you,' she whispered shakily, willing him to draw it into himself and accept it completely. 'More than you will ever know. You are my sun and moon, my reason for living. I'm only half alive when I'm not with you.'

But even as they kissed again, still locked together in an embrace as old and elemental as time, she wondered if he would ever really understand and learn to trust.

Marianne left the bedsit that evening for good, but contrary to what she expected Zeke did not drive to the apartment.

It took her a good twenty minutes to realise where they were heading for, but as they approached Hertfordshire she understood, her hand reaching out to grip Zeke's as the lump in her throat prevented her from speaking. He was taking her to the house.

'The apartment's gone.' He stopped the car at the top of the common for a moment or two, turning to her as he spoke. 'The furniture, everything. I thought we needed a new start.'

'When?' She was very near breaking point with all the emotion of the last few hours and the realisation that the terrible isolation and loneliness of the last weeks and months was over.

'I put it on the market the day after I did this,' he said quietly, gesturing at his ankle. 'That last misunderstanding between us... It seemed to signify how things had been there. You never liked it, did you?'

'No,' she said softly, her eyes glinting with unshed tears. 'I never did.'

'It sold in twenty-four hours.' Zeke was looking straight ahead now, towards the big Victorian whitewashed house that was their new home. 'Which gave me a few weeks to get things sorted here. Of course you can make any changes you see fit,' he added as he pressed down on the accelerator.

Marianne sat quite still as the car purred along the road running parallel with the common, and then they were turning through big gates and on to the drive of the house she had fallen in love with all those months ago.

Her heart was thudding in her chest and she felt weak at the knees, although she wasn't quite sure why. When she had spoken to the Bedlows on her visit in November they had been quite willing to sell any of their beautiful antique furniture Marianne wanted; their house in Portugal was already furnished as it had been their holiday home for the last five years.

She had loved some of the mellow old pieces and had tentatively chosen what she would like to retain, although then, in the back of her mind, she had wondered if they would suit Zeke after the stylish modernness of the apartment.

The first things she saw as she entered the large, sloping-

roofed porch were the two white Lloyd Loom chairs and
the small cane table, and she turned to Zeke, her eyes
shining.

'Oh, Zeke! You kept these.'

They had been hand in hand, but now he whisked her
up into his arms, his eyes tender and his mouth hungry as
he kissed her until she was breathless before saying, 'The
Bedlows assured me you liked them. Now, prepare to be
carried over the threshold, wench,' he added smilingly.

'Mind your ankle!'

He had been limping quite badly—their sexual gymnas-
tics at the bedsit couldn't have been beneficial to a newly
healed bone, and neither could the drive to the house—but
from the scathing glance he bestowed on her she wisely
decided to say nothing more.

'Oh, it's just as I remember,' she said delightedly.

He had kissed her again before placing her on her feet
in the hall, and now, as she gazed at the beautifully carved
staircase and mellow wood floor, she felt as though she
was dreaming.

This morning she had been counting the pennies to see
if she had enough money for the tube as well as some
photocopying she needed at the library, and tonight... Tonight she was in paradise.

It was when Zeke opened the door to the drawing room
that she knew she was going to cry, in spite of all her
efforts to the contrary. The pale green and warm buttery-
yellow colour scheme was exactly in line with her
sketches, and every piece of furniture she had wanted to
keep was there, along with a few new pieces that fitted
perfectly.

'How...?' She turned to find him watching her very
closely, and she wondered how she could ever have
thought his grey eyes cold.

'I just followed your ideas,' he said softly, 'but you can change anything you don't like.'

'I love it.' She flung her arms around his neck, suddenly petrified that this was a dream and she would wake up and he would be gone. She held on to him tightly, burying her face in his broad chest as she sought the reassurance of his solidness.

'We'll make it work,' he promised thickly above her head as he sensed her panic. 'This is a new beginning, my love.'

My love. She pressed even closer, a nameless dread filling her soul for a moment. He called her his love and she believed he meant it, but was he really able to change? Really able to trust her, to believe that she meant to grow old with him, love him, cherish and adore him? He had admitted he wasn't there yet, and until he was they would never really be happy.

And then she brushed the chill away, resolutely lifting her face for his kiss. She would *make* him understand, whatever it took. She didn't think she could go through the last few months again and survive. She needed him just as much as he needed her.

The rest of the house was just as she had envisaged, although apart from the master bedroom the other rooms upstairs were unfurnished as yet, with just the odd piece from the Bedlows dotted about although all the carpets and curtains had been left.

They sat up into the early hours making plans, and then they went to bed, to lie in each other's arms and love until dawn was breaking over a night-washed sky and the birds were singing in the garden below. *Their* garden, she thought wonderingly.

Sunday was spent mostly in bed, and Monday morning Zeke called in to the office to say he was taking the day off, but gradually life resumed some sort of normality.

Marianne continued at the supermarket for a further few days until Mrs Polinkski's daughter—who had delayed her departure from Poland several times—returned home, and then she threw herself into furnishing the rest of the house.

Zeke left later in the mornings and returned earlier in the evenings, often mid-afternoon, and one or two evenings Marianne took the bull by the horns and spread out the college and university prospectuses and showed him the courses she was considering.

He was encouraging at those times, but restrained, and when she invited Pat down for the weekend of their third week in Hertfordshire he left them alone on the Saturday, to have a good chin-wag, and then took both girls out to dinner in the evening and behaved impeccably towards Pat, who, albeit reluctantly at first, was won over.

'You set out to charm her, didn't you?' Marianne accused that night as they got ready for bed, her eyes brimming with laughter at the smug expression on his handsome face. 'You can be a smooth devil when you want to be, Zeke Buchanan.'

'I don't deny it.' He grinned at her, his eyes dancing, and her own smile widened. He seemed lighter these days, freer, and she passionately wanted to believe it would last.

It was all going to be all right, she told herself as she lay beside him later that night, listening to his steady breathing. He was accepting the thought of her studying for a degree now, had actually discussed her choices of university with Pat and herself at dinner, and it had been he who had suggested they go and spend the weekend with her father in a couple of weeks' time and include Pat again when they went out for dinner.

He had dismissed the apartment and city life without a qualm, and he seemed—he *seemed*—to enjoy living on the outskirts and being at home more. But how did she know for sure?

She wriggled slightly, angry with herself, but she couldn't help it. He had told her, the first night at the house, that he had come face to face with himself that lunch-time he had seen her with Wilmer and realised he was poised on the edge of a chasm.

'You said I'd ruin your life as well as mine if I didn't get a handle on this thing.' She had been clasped in his arms and he had moved her slightly to look down into her uplifted face. 'It was like a bolt of lightning, Marianne, I can't explain it. In everything that had happened I'd never grasped that before,' he had admitted soberly.

'Because you'd never understood how much I love you?' she had asked gently. 'Is that why?'

'I don't know. Perhaps. But the shock of first seeing you with him, the look on his face—I thought for a moment I had lost you. And then you declared your love for me again... It was like a second chance. And then I got angry.'

'With me?' she had asked, with careful neutrality.

'With myself. The problem was mine and yet I was making you shoulder it. It wasn't fair,' he'd said with a touch of grimness. 'None of this has been fair.'

'Neither was your childhood,' she'd murmured softly, holding him, loving him so much it hurt.

He'd shrugged, tracing a path round the outline of her soft lips with a tender finger. 'People endure worse without letting it cripple them,' he'd said quietly. 'I sat in the taxi and looked down at my ankle and realised there were worse ways of being crippled than by broken bones. I'd always prided myself on being a fighter, on seeing problems merely as embryo opportunities, so where was that warrior spirit over this?'

They had talked some more, and she had been reassured at the time, but since then little niggling doubts—born of the long months apart and the misery of the last year at the apartment—had crept in much as she had tried to dismiss them.

She wouldn't allow them any more headroom. She stared fiercely into the darkness, willing the panic and unease to leave. Zeke was too intuitive by half, and if he sensed she was doubting him it could seriously jeopardise this new understanding between them which was still so sweet.

She had told him he had to trust her and the boot was just as relevant on the other foot, too! She wouldn't think another negative thought. He deserved all her faith for their future.

Nevertheless, it was some time before she fell into a restless slumber, and her dreams were full of nightmarish images and long dark corridors that stretched endlessly into oblivion.

Marianne awoke late the next morning and she lay for some time without moving, in the grip of a deep, all-embracing weariness that seemed a little extreme for the couple of hours' sleep she had missed. Nevertheless her limbs felt like lead.

It was Saturday morning, and in the distance somewhere she could hear church bells, and the faint murmur of voices downstairs, which she assumed was Zeke and Pat, Zeke's side of the bed being empty. She really ought to go and join them, she thought tiredly.

She forced herself to sit up, feeling guilty she hadn't been downstairs when Pat went down, and then felt so horribly ill she thought she was going to faint. She sank back against the pillows before she realised she had to get to the bathroom as a wave of nausea swept over her, but a few minutes later, once she was minus the contents of her stomach, she began to feel a little better and struggled back to bed.

'Marianne?' She had just slid under the covers when Zeke walked in the door with a cup of tea in his hand, the smile which had been on his face fading as he took in her ghostly pallor. 'What's wrong, darling? Are you ill?'

'I feel awful.' It was something of a plaintive wail but she *hated* being sick. 'It must be a tummy bug or something.'

Zeke immediately took charge, ordering her to stay in bed and rest and assuring her that he and Pat were quite capable of seeing to the Sunday dinner between them. However, by lunch-time she felt as right as rain, and joined the other two downstairs for a big meal of roast beef, Yorkshire pudding and three veg, which she ate with gusto.

The three of them went for walk in the afternoon, calling in at a small oak-beamed thatched pub on the way home, before Pat left for Bridgeton with promises she'd be up to see them again soon.

Marianne slept heavily that night, and was barely awake when Zeke kissed her goodbye in the morning after placing a cup of tea on her bedside cabinet.

Within moments of sitting up in bed she had to run for the bathroom in a repeat of yesterday's performance, but this time a disturbing possibility had her stomach turning upside down long after the nausea had subsided. But she couldn't be. Could she?

By mid-morning her suspicions were confirmed after a visit to the local chemist for a pregnancy testing kit. She was trembling as she sat at the kitchen table staring at the little vial, myriad emotions jumbling her thoughts and causing her head to swim. A baby. Zeke's baby. They had started a new life.

She had put the non-appearance of her monthly cycle after Christmas down to stress, remembering all the other times in the past when she had been two, three, even four weeks late. And then when Zeke had come for her and literally swept her off her feet again she just hadn't thought of it in all the excitement of furnishing the house. And why should she? All their careful following of charts and such in the last year of their marriage had produced nothing; pregnancy was the last thing—the very last thing—that would have crossed her mind.

But she *was* pregnant and it was Zeke's baby growing inside her. Her hand moved protectively to her stomach and she shut her eyes tightly, her mind racing.

How could you be thrilled and scared to death at the same time? she asked herself weakly. A baby was wonderful, the fulfilment of all the dreams and longings she had felt for so long, *but it was the wrong time.*

She opened her eyes, staring vacantly round the beautiful kitchen as she brushed a strand of hair out of her eyes with a shaking hand.

It was too soon—far, far too soon for Zeke. He had just begun to accept the idea of her going to university and working for a career, of her being with other people and following her own star to a limited extent. This pregnancy would be the end of all that, certainly for a few years at least, and she had never liked the idea of having just one child anyway. Two, or even three, had always been her heart's desire, and close in ages so they could enjoy each other, as she would have loved to have been able to enjoy the company of a sister or a brother.

This pregnancy would satisfy all the possessive darkness of his strange nature; he wouldn't be able to resist falling back into his old ways—it was like a gift from the gods. A destructive, self-indulgent gift.

No, no, she couldn't think of their baby like that. She shook her head, a little moan escaping her white lips. And, whatever, she wanted this baby more than anything in the world. It would mean the world to Zeke; he would be thrilled to bits. It was just that if it had happened a few years from now, when he had really come to terms with his jealousy, it would have been so much better for them. She was frightened, terribly frightened of how their relationship would suffer.

She spent the rest of the day in a state of fermenting unrest. She had been feeling increasingly tired lately, she recognised when she thought about it, almost drained at times. And the non-appearance of the physical signs should have alerted her long before this. But what difference would it have made? She could have insisted they remain apart during her pregnancy, given him more time to conquer his personal demons, she answered herself.

But, no, that wouldn't have worked, she reasoned in the next moment. She couldn't have lived apart from him at a time like this, not loving him with all her heart and carrying their child.

But perhaps that sacrifice would have been worth it in the long run if it helped him master the distrust and fear that had nearly wrecked their marriage and tormented him so? Would she have the strength and determination a few years from now, even possibly a decade or more, to reach out for that career that was becoming more and more distant? Would it mean fighting him again, and this time with a family to consider?

The questions and answers, and counter-questions and answers went on all day, and by the time Zeke arrived home, just as an early dusk was turning the sky pink and gold, she was mentally and physically exhausted.

She had phoned the local surgery that afternoon and booked an appointment with the doctor, but by her own calculations she thought she was eleven weeks pregnant or thereabouts, although she wasn't absolutely sure of her dates. Ten, eleven, twelve weeks—what did it matter? she asked herself wryly. She was well and truly pregnant, and a week or so was neither here or there.

'What's all this?' She had met Zeke at the door and led him straight into the dining room, where she had set a romantic table with their best crystal and cutlery, two candles already lit and a bowl of fresh flowers perfuming the air. 'I haven't missed something, have I? It isn't your birthday or our anniversary, and I know my birthday was in June.' He grinned at her, his face open and warm, and she forced herself to smile back.

'There's some champagne on ice in the kitchen.' She was prevaricating, she knew it, but now the moment was here she just didn't seem able to get the words out. She felt elated and wildly excited on the one hand, and terrified on the other, and added to that distinctly light-headed. In all her agitation she had forgotten to eat lunch.

'Champagne?' His grey eyes had narrowed on her flushed face and now there was a touch of wariness in their smoky depths. 'Do I take it this is a celebration? What have you done?'

'Not me. Well, not just me,' she said shakily, her love for him suddenly overwhelming her. He was going to be so pleased and that was all that mattered. He deserved a family; he deserved every bit of love he got after the misery of his childhood, she told herself vehemently. And whatever happened in the future, however difficult things got, she must remember that. And he would be a brilliant, *fantastic* father.

'I'm all ears.' He was still smiling but she sensed it was with some effort. 'Fire away.'

'I'm pregnant,' she said simply.

'What?' The stunned amazement was absolute. 'What did you say?'

'You're going to be a father. That time it snowed—' She didn't manage to get anything more out before he had reached her, swinging her up into his arms as he said, 'Marianne. Oh, my love, my love,' in between showering her face with kisses. She was astounded to see his eyes were wet.

And then she cried, and they held each other close, pressed together for a small eternity as he stroked her hair and kissed her and said beautiful things she knew she would treasure all her life.

The meal she had cooked was wonderful, and when, later that night, he made love to her, it was with an exquisite gentleness he had never shown before.

Everything was fine.

She lay enfolded in his arms as they drifted off to sleep and it was her last conscious thought. It was. Everything was fine. She didn't question why she had to repeat it over and over again.

In the morning she was sick again, and Zeke wouldn't be prised from her side, only leaving the house mid-morning when she was feeling herself once more. He had sat on the bed, insisting she have a cup of tea and a couple of dry biscuits before she attempted to get up, and they had talked about the baby, which room would be good for a nursery, how perfect the house was for children, the nearness of schools—everything but her degree.

It was the same that evening, and for the next few days, and as time went on Marianne's apprehension grew. It was as though she had never proposed going to university, never wanted a career, she thought desperately. He saw her chained to the house now. Wife and mother, nothing more. They were back at the beginning.

Of course she could have brought the subject up herself, but something deep inside balked at that. If he went cold again, remote, she wouldn't be able to stand it, besides which she didn't want him to think she wasn't as thrilled about their baby as he was. She was over the moon, ecstatic, but so fearful for him. For them.

On Friday morning she kept her appointment with the doctor, who turned out to be a small round barrel of a man with the gentlest brown eyes she had ever seen.

He asked her the normal, somewhat impersonal questions relating to her condition and examined her briefly, stating that the dates she mentioned matched the twelve-week-old foetus he could feel. And then he sat back in his seat, his kind gaze very direct as he said, 'You seem troubled, Mrs Buchanan. Edgy. Are you worried about having this baby?'

'No, not really, not the baby. At least...' Her voice trailed away and she looked at him miserably over the big polished desk. Where did she start to explain? she asked herself silently.

'Yes?' he prompted gently. 'What's wrong, Mrs Buchanan?'

'My husband and I only recently got back together after being separated for a few months,' she said awkwardly, and then, as she caught his expression, added hastily, 'But the baby is his; that's not the issue. It's just... Well, I'm not sure if we're ready to have a child. Not that either of us would consider not having it; we're both over the moon...' She paused again. She wasn't explaining this very well.

'Have you told him how you feel?' the doctor asked quietly.

'No.' She flushed a little. 'It's nothing, really. I'm probably being silly.' She couldn't explain the whole complicated mess to a stranger and suddenly she just wanted to leave.

He must have sensed how she felt, because he became very brisk and businesslike, but then, just as she was leaving, he said carefully, 'This is a very important time for you, Mrs Buchanan, and you need all the support your husband is able to give you. Talk to him, eh?'

She swallowed, and then nodded slowly. She had got more and more keyed up as the week had progressed, and that couldn't be good for the baby, could it? Zeke had buried his feelings for the first two years of their marriage and look what that lack of communication had resulted in. She needed to air her misgivings, or at least broach the subject if he didn't intend to. It was the only way.

She drove home with her mind only half on the road and the traffic, and once in the house fixed herself a light lunch of cold meat and salad which she ate at the kitchen table.

Since their reunion Zeke had taken to arriving home early on a Friday afternoon, often before three, but by five there was still no sign of him and she found herself getting worried.

She had lit the fire in the pretty floral sitting room after lunch, pulling the sofa close to the crackling flames and dozing on and off most of the murky, overcast February afternoon, but at five she was wide awake, looking out into the dark garden as the storm which had been threatening all day began to break in the heavens.

Lightning was flashing across the sky, great jagged streaks which silhouetted the ebony thunderclouds with silver. An icy cold wind was moaning about the house, lashing the trees and bushes into a frenzy now and again and causing the odd billow of smoke from the fire in the grate.

Marianne shivered, although the sitting room was as warm as toast, and wandered through to the front of the house to stand looking out of the drawing room windows at the empty drive for some minutes, before returning again to the warmth and cosiness of the sitting room.

Was this storm an omen? she asked herself silently. A portent of what was to come if she opened Pandora's box?

They were supposed to be going out to dinner tonight; Zeke had reserved a table at a local restaurant which had an excellent reputation and cost a small fortune, and they were due to arrive for seven.

If he was much later she would have to leave talking to him until they returned home. She didn't want to rush the conversation or leave for the restaurant halfway through; it was too important.

Zeke phoned five minutes later and he sounded harassed.

'Sorry, I'm going to be late,' he said quickly. 'I'll explain when I see you. Could you be ready to leave when I get home, which should be about half past six?'

'Of course.' She kept her voice bright and steady as she battled with the thought—quite unfair, she admitted silently—that he was reverting to how it had been before she had left him. He had often arrived home late then, content in the knowledge she would be waiting for him in her glass tower.

But it wasn't like that now, she told herself firmly after she had said goodbye and replaced the receiver. And he was running a multimillion-pound business, for goodness' sake; there were going to be some days which weren't plain sailing and necessitated long hours.

Nevertheless, the feeling of *déjà vu* persisted all the time she was getting ready, and several times her hand moved to the faint mound of her stomach as though seeking some kind of reassurance.

She stood staring at herself when she was ready for some moments. The off-the-shoulder cashmere top in deep violet teamed beautifully with the pencil-slim skirt ending in frivolous frills just below her knees. It wouldn't be long before she wouldn't be able to wear her normal clothes, she told herself with what she realised was a little dart of sheer pleasure. She was looking forward to seeing her stomach grow, knowing it was Zeke's child she was carrying, although no doubt by the end of nine months she would be heartily glad to return to her normal shape.

Zeke roared on to the drive at a quarter to seven, and she was just slipping into her coat when he opened the front door. 'You look gorgeous.' He ran his hands down her body under the coat as he pulled her close for a long moment and kissed her. 'Good enough to eat.'

So did he. She smiled into the handsome aesthetic face, feeling the power that radiated out from him with a frisson of sensual pleasure. He had always had a devastating presence; it went with the cold, arrogant good looks and the air of command that was as natural to him as breathing.

It would be so easy to lose her own identity, she thought soberly a moment later as they walked out to the car. To be smothered, taken over, as she had nearly been in the past. And then she brushed the thought away, determined to enjoy the evening out with the man she loved and the father of her baby. Later was later, and she would say what needed to be said then. For now she wanted to drench herself in the pleasure of being with him.

The restaurant was fabulous: discreet lighting, beautiful surroundings—it even had a miniature waterfall in one corner and a pianist in full evening dress in another, providing a melodious background to the buzz of conversation emanating from the assembled diners.

The food was everything they had been promised it would be; the mousseline of smoked salmon with asparagus and saffron dressing melted in her mouth and the fricassee of chicken with tarragon and wild mushroom sauce was truly delicious, but it was the dessert—silver-dusted double chocolate torte with whipped cream—that was the supreme triumph of the evening as far as Marianne was concerned.

'That was truly gorgeous.' Marianne curled back in her

seat like a small satisfied cat as she spooned the last delicious mouthful in her mouth, and raised her eyes to see
Zeke watching her, an amused quirk to his mouth.

'Come tomorrow morning you won't be feeling so
pleased with yourself,' he warned softly, laughing out loud
as she pouted at him for the bad taste of the remark.

'I daren't come here too often,' she said lightly. 'I'm
going to be fat enough as it is.'

'You're going to be beautiful and desirable.' His voice
was husky and very warm.

'Will you still say that when you come home to tired,
grizzly children, a house cluttered with hundreds of toys
and an irritable wife who hasn't had time to do her hair?'
she teased softly.

'Ah…' He surveyed her from dark glittering eyes. 'Now
that brings me very neatly on to something I've been looking into over the last few days, and the main reason why
I was late tonight. I needed to pay a visit to one or two
medical establishments.'

She stared at him, puzzled at his tone. It was one of
suppressed excitement and eagerness.

'We're going to have a baby,' he continued softly.
'Right?'

'It's definitely more than a bout of indigestion!' She
grinned at him, the excellent meal and one glass of wine
she had allowed herself giving her something of a devil-
may-care feeling that was wonderfully liberating after all
the agitation and soul-searching of the last few days.

'Our baby.' He hadn't returned her smile, and now she
found herself searching his face. 'Yours and mine.'

'Zeke?' She was beginning to feel panicky and she
didn't like it.

'Agreed?' he pressed, still in the same low voice.

'Of course it's your baby and mine.' She didn't have a

clue where he was coming from, but something was afoot, and the smile had died.

'Do you know that with your standard of A level passes a hospital laboratory would be prepared to accept you as a trainee?' Zeke asked mildly. 'You'd be given exemption from some of the National Certificate exam in chemistry and biology, but there'd be a few years attending day-release and evening classes with all manner of further exams to pass. Of course there'd be the asset of working in a laboratory, which would enable you to learn useful practical skills, but with all the out of work study and so on you'd be working all the hours under the sun.'

She was too amazed to say a word.

'So, although that seemed a good idea on the face of it, I don't think it's great for you in your current position, not now the baby has changed things.'

'Zeke—' She took a deep breath. This was so surreal. 'When did you start looking into all this?' she asked shakily.

'A couple of weeks ago,' he answered quietly, his grey eyes tight on her bewildered face. 'I knew how much you wanted to work in a laboratory so I wanted to explore all the options before you committed absolutely to a straightforward degree. Once I'd got all the facts and figures I was going to discuss it with you and we could have decided what was right for us.'

If a choir of angels had suddenly materialised singing 'Hosanna in the Highest' Marianne couldn't have been more astounded. He had been investigating a job for her, she thought dazedly, wondering if her ears were deceiving her.

'But now it looks as though we're back to the university idea,' Zeke continued evenly, 'which should be fine as long as we can get you into somewhere near, so you don't have to drive too far on the days you need to attend lectures and so on.'

'You mean now, in the immediate future after the baby's born?' she asked in surprise. 'Are you suggesting we have a nanny?'

'We could get a nanny.' He eyed her stolidly, enjoying the utter bemusement she couldn't hide. 'But I don't fancy a stranger living with us, somehow, and however dedicated she would be she wouldn't love it as we will. So on the days you're at university I'll be at home, okay?'

'What?'

'We'll share caring for our child between us,' he said coolly, his handsome face calm. 'You told me once I could delegate and you're right, I can. I've got over six months to set it all up, and we can turn the breakfast room into a joint study for both of us. It looks out on to the garden, and with the big French windows it's perfect.'

'But, but your work…' Marianne couldn't take her eyes off his face. 'Buchanan Industries…'

'I own Buchanan Industries; I can do whatever I want,' he said drily. 'What's the point of being the boss if you can't call the tune? I don't want to miss seeing my children grow up.'

'Do you mean it? Do you really want to do this?' she asked softly, the fierce emotion that was growing and growing inside her making her voice tremble.

'Yes,' he said huskily. 'We'll take it as it comes, Marianne, over the years. We'll have our family, God willing, and we'll have each other and that will be the main thing. We'll see our children growing up, surrounded by love, and with two happy, fulfilled parents who love them and each other. It might not be the traditional way of doing things but it will be our way, and we can always get additional help later if we need it.'

The tears were blocking her throat, but she still managed

to murmur, 'You don't have to do this, Zeke. I know how important your work is to you. I can stay at home for a few years and then go to college when the children are all at school.'

'You're important to me,' he corrected softly, reaching for her hand and lifting it to his mouth, kissing it tenderly. 'We'll share our careers and our children and our grandchildren. We'll make our house ring with laughter and joy, and the kids will never know what it feels like to be unwanted or unloved. They'll grow and blossom and become anything they want to be, like their mother.'

She looked at him, her love so intense it hurt. 'I love you,' she whispered mistily. 'I love you with all my heart.'

'I know.'

His face was open, his grey eyes perfectly at peace and filled with a light that had banished all the darkness.

They had come through, they were together in heart and mind, and it was only going to get better in the years to come. This was the greatest thing in all the world. This was love.

The Dysarts

A family with a passion for life—and for love.

by *Catherine George*

Get to know the Dysarts!

Over the coming months, you can share the dramas and joys, and hopes and dreams of this wealthy English family, as unexpected passions, births and marriages unfold in their lives.

Look out for…

RESTLESS NIGHTS

Harlequin Presents® #2244
on-sale April 2002

and

SWEET SURRENDER

Harlequin Presents® #2285
on-sale November 2002

The world's bestselling romance series.

Coming Next Month

HARLEQUIN *Presents*

THE BEST HAS JUST GOTTEN BETTER!

#2241 THE WEDDING ULTIMATUM Helen Bianchin
Danielle D'Alboa faces bankruptcy and is forced to appeal to Rafael Valdez, the Spanish tycoon, for help. He has a proposal: marry him and produce an heir and all her debts will be cleared! Danielle has twenty-four hours to decide....

#2242 THE SECRET LOVE-CHILD Miranda Lee
Rafe wanted Isabel. But his job was to photograph the bride-to-be, not seduce her. Then he discovered the wedding was off and Isabel boldly asked him to accompany her on what would have been her honeymoon....

#2243 THE PREGNANT MISTRESS Sandra Marton
Greek tycoon Demetrios Karas is in danger of blowing a whole business deal if he doesn't make his translator, Samantha Brewster, his mistress. But Samantha seems willing to stay only until the end of her three-month contract....

#2244 RESTLESS NIGHTS Catherine George
Gabriel is a girl of independence, happy with her career in London. But when Adam Dysart strides back into her life, his charisma turns her balanced emotions to jelly! Gabriel knows if she lets him into her life, she'll let him into her bed, too....

#2245 THE BOSS'S PROPOSAL Cathy Williams
Vicky's relationship with Max Forbes, her sexy new boss, had to stay strictly business—just in case he discovered her secret. But after a passionate night together, Max came face-to-face with Chloe, Vicky's young daughter, and the secret was out....

#2246 THE DEVIL'S BARGAIN Robyn Donald
Hope had refused to succumb to Keir Carmichael's charm five years ago and had set off instead to travel Australia. But when Keir walks into her workplace, all suave sophistication and dark, stunning looks, Hope's emotions are thrown into confusion....